'You're not married?'

Patrick looked down at his bare left hand, absently stroking the place where his wedding band, gone for almost three years now, had sat. 'Not any more.'

Miranda, conscious of the occasional brush of his arm and the heat radiating from his thigh to hers, almost sagged against him in relief. She might not be experienced at picking up men in bars, and it certainly hadn't been her intent when she came to the symposium, but she was pretty sure there was an undercurrent between them.

An undercurrent she probably would never have explored under normal circumstances. But Lola was at a sleepover and, thanks to the generosity of her grandmother, she was staying the night at a swanky hotel.

And she was extraordinarily attracted to Patrick Costello. And, if she wasn't very much mistaken, the feeling was mutual.

This wasn't some seventeen-year-old girl crush. This was all grown-up. And she wanted it. Her pulse tripped at the thought of doing something a little reckless for a change.

She drained the remnants of her glass. Maybe she could have one crazy night?

'Would you like another wine?' he asked.

Miranda met his gaze, felt it rove over her face and settle on her mouth. She'd been a single mother since she was seventeen. She wasn't up on the rules of this situation. But the part of her that was female, that responded to his maleness, knew that another wine implied so much more than just a second glass.

If she was sensible she'd walk away right now.

But she was so tired of always being sensible.

She lifted her chin and looked straight into his golden-brown eyes. 'Yes, please.'

Dear Reader

Don't you just love stories about people who really want to be together but can't? The yearning and the tension and the will they/won't they conundrum as the story evolves and you know something's gotta give. I think it's especially touching when children are involved. When two people who are obviously attracted to each other deny it so they can be good parents to their children.

Except we all know how that one's going to end, right?

Parents are people too and surely a man and a woman who have always done the right thing and strived through difficult circumstances to be there and be everything for their kids, deserve a little happiness?

I hope you'll agree that Patrick and Miranda do. Ruby and Lola, their little girls, certainly do.

From their first meeting in a hotel lift to their eventual HEA there aren't two more worthy people than Patrick and Miranda.

I hope you enjoy their story.

Love,

Amy

ONE NIGHT SHE WOULD NEVER FORGET

BY
AMY ANDREWS

MILLS
BOON

First published in Great Britain 2013
by Mills & Boon, an imprint of Harlequin (UK) Limited,
Large Print edition 2013
Harlequin (UK) Limited, Eton House,
18-24 Paradise Road, Richmond, Surrey TW9 1SR

© Amy Andrews 2013

ISBN: 978 0 263 23149 6

Harlequin (UK) policy is to use papers that are natural, renewable and recyclable products and made from wood grown in sustainable forests. The logging and manufacturing process conform to the legal environmental regulations of the country of origin.

Printed and bound in Great Britain
by CPI Antony Rowe, Chippenham, Wiltshire

DEDICATION:

For Ethan, Saul, Quinn, Neve and Jem—
an aunt couldn't ask for nicer nieces and nephews!

Amy Andrews has always loved writing, and still can't quite believe that she gets to do it for a living. Creating wonderful heroines and gorgeous heroes and telling their stories is an amazing way to pass the day. Sometimes they don't always act as she'd like them to—but then neither do her kids, so she's kind of used to it. Amy lives in the very beautiful Samford Valley, with her husband and aforementioned children, along with six brown chooks and two black dogs. She loves to hear from her readers. Drop her a line at www.amyandrews.com.au

Recent titles by the same author:

SYDNEY HARBOUR HOSPITAL:
  EVIE'S BOMBSHELL*
HOW TO MEND A BROKEN HEART
SYDNEY HARBOUR HOSPITAL:
  LUCA'S BAD GIRL*
WAKING UP WITH DR OFF-LIMITS
JUST ONE LAST NIGHT…
RESCUED BY THE DREAMY DOC
VALENTINO'S PREGNANCY BOMBSHELL
ALLESANDRO AND THE CHEERY NANNY

Sydney Harbour Hospital

These books are also available in eBook format from www.millsandboon.co.uk

CHAPTER ONE

September

MIRANDA DEAN PAID no heed to the man getting into the lift as she searched through her bag for her room key. This was the problem with having bags big enough to throw a party in—you could never find anything.

Why hadn't she just slotted it into the back of the nametag holder hanging around her neck, like everyone else?

She felt a nudge at her elbow and a deep voice asking, 'Yours?'

She looked up to see a fluffy pink miniature teddy in the palm of a big tanned hand. *Pinky!*

'Oh, yes, thank you,' she murmured, reaching for the toy that looked particularly girly in stark contrast to the very male hand.

Her gaze wandered higher, and higher, a grateful smile on her face for the finder of such a precious item. Her breath caught at the very sexy man who smiled back. He looked tired. Lines around his eyes, tie pulled askew, unshaven jaw, dark, rumpled hair suffering from a bad case of finger-combing, but his gaze was lit with laughter, and the dimple in his chin? Well, that was plain sinful.

Not to mention the intoxicating scent of him spicing the air around her.

'You take it everywhere you go?' he teased as he relinquished the object then buried his hand in his pocket.

Miranda blushed as the humorous note in his voice did strange things to her equilibrium. Was he…flirting with her? Or just being nice?

She really didn't have enough practice with this kind of thing.

'It's not mine…it's Lola's,' she clarified. Well, attempted to anyway but obviously failed as one nice thick manly eyebrow kicked up. 'My daughter's…Lola is my daughter,' she explained, her fingers stroking absently along the soft pink satin patches delineating Pinky's paws. 'She's four… well, nearly five actually… She's not with me…'

she ended lamely, wishing the lift doors would just open already before she sounded any more socially inept.

The universe obliged.

'This is my stop,' she prattled, apparently now unable to stop with the talking.

He smiled at her and Miranda wished she could tell if he was amused with her or by her. 'Me too,' he murmured, and indicated for Miranda to precede him.

Excellent! Somehow her legs kicked into gear and she exited, aware of him falling in beside her. Aware of his height and his breadth and the way he moderated his long-legged stride to match hers. Aware of his scent again—spicy man times ten with an end note of sweetness that tickled her senses.

And her hormones.

'So…you're at the conference?' he asked.

Miranda nodded, dragging her brain away from the alluring smell of him. She'd been thrilled when the hospital had sponsored her, a lowly new grad, to attend the two-day international medical symposium being held in Brisbane for the first time ever. It had been a veritable smorgasbord of exciting new information. 'You?' she asked.

He nodded. 'I'm presenting a paper tomorrow.'

Miranda's step faltered. Good lord, she'd been prattling on like a mad woman about a pink teddy to some hotshot bigwig! She was probably supposed to know who he was on sight.

'Oh,' she said absently, as her brain busily flicked through the programme pages she'd consulted about a hundred times that day, trying to place him.

He chuckled. 'I promise it's not that boring.'

Miranda turned to him as they walked, reaching for his arm automatically and touching it briefly. 'Oh, no.' She shook her head. 'I'm sorry… I didn't mean it like that. I—'

He chuckled again and she could see he was teasing her once more. She almost sagged against him in relief. 'You mock.'

He smiled back at her in reply and Miranda's legs suddenly felt as if they were filled with jelly. It was the kind of smile that could make her forget she was a single working mother of a four-nearly-five-year-old. That could make her wonder what it might be like to have his wicked looking mouth on hers.

It really ought to be illegal to smile in such a way.

She was grateful when her room loomed and she could break away from the pull of him. It was titillating and unnerving in equal parts. She wasn't in a position to give in to her weak knees or to the butterflies in her belly.

Why, suddenly, did that feel like a regret?

'This is me,' she announced as she stopped at her door.

He smiled that illegal smile again and said, 'We're neighbours. I hope you don't snore.'

Miranda felt her stomach turn over several times. He needn't worry about that. She probably wouldn't get to sleep at all now! 'I've had no complaints.'

The humour that had sparkled in his eyes morphed into a rich glitter as Miranda realised what she'd said.

Dear God—had she taken a stupid pill?

Now the man probably thought her mattress was a veritable hotbed of vice. Which couldn't be further from the truth. The only pleasure she'd got there in years had been an extra lie-in on Sunday mornings—if she was lucky!

'Ah…okay…that came out all wrong,' she said.

Why she felt the urge to put it straight she had no idea. The man already knew she had a daughter, he surely didn't expect her to be a virgin. And, anyway, what the hell did it matter what he thought? He didn't know her—they'd only just met, for crying out loud.

He looked at her for a prolonged moment and Miranda felt her nipples bead against her bra as the heat from his gaze fanned over her. 'Sounded okay to me,' he murmured. Then he inclined his head and ambled off, throwing, 'Goodnight, Miranda,' over his shoulder.

Miranda? She stared after him. *He knew her name*? She stood unmoving by her door, watching him take the five paces to his door and then reach inside his jacket pocket for his key.

'How do you…know my name?'

He turned towards her, shoving his biceps against the door and giving her that smile again. Like he could see right through her clothes to the knot her knickers were tying themselves into.

He pointed at her chest and said, 'Your nametag.'

Miranda looked down. The item in question swung slightly against her breasts from the movement. 'Oh.'

He grinned. 'Happy dreams.'

And by the time she looked up again, his door was clicking shut.

Patrick Costello flopped fully clothed back on his bed, a smile on his face. Four nights of interrupted sleep—three with an ill child and last night in the operating theatre with a kidney transplant—had left him utterly wrecked.

But Miranda Dean's cute little blush had perked him up considerably.

He lay in the dark, the lights off, staring at the ceiling. *It was so quiet.* The low hum of the air-con was all that could be heard in the well-insulated room and it was unnerving. Back home in suburban Sydney he was surrounded by the constant chatter of a four-year-old and the blare of the television as his mother-in-law settled in for her nightly shows.

Silence was a novelty.

It should be bliss, he supposed, but it just felt wrong. It always felt wrong when he was away from Ruby.

He sat up and flicked the television on, clicking the remote until he came to a news station. But the noise wasn't the same and the room felt cold and empty.

He wondered if it felt like that next door. Was Miranda missing her daughter too?

He'd noticed her as soon as the lift doors had opened—hard not to as she had been the only occupant. But he'd have noticed her through a crowd with that curtain of wavy ebony hair falling forward as she trawled through her voluminous bag. A sleek navy skirt with fine pinstripes clung to hips and thighs that could only belong to a woman. A glossy dark grey blouse fell against very nice breasts, her nametag swinging enticingly between them.

Miranda Dean.

Did she always carry the little pink teddy or was it just one of those things that seemed to find their way into bags when a child was in the mix?

Interesting that she too had a four-year-old daughter.

Very interesting.

He caught himself smiling again and groaned as he flopped back. *Get a grip.* You have a presentation to embellish and sleep to catch up on.

Now have a shower and get to work!

Patrick obeyed the stern voice in his head, knowing it was right. He wasn't here to swap baby photos and funny kiddie stories with a woman he barely knew just because he was missing Ruby. It was only one night and two days. He could get by without mentioning her name, surely?

He jumped in the shower, dunking himself under the spray, washing away some of the exhaustion but knowing no matter how long he stayed it could never wash away the accumulated hours of lost sleep and worry over the last four-plus years.

They went bone deep.

He got out, dried off, ruffled his damp hair, pulled on some jeans, snagged a beer out of the fridge and headed for the desk, the flickering light from the television guiding the way. He switched on the desk lamp as he sat and opened his laptop then took a deep swallow of his beer and got to work.

Two hours later he'd checked his emails, added some slides to his presentation and done some literature reviews for a new study he and three other anaesthetists were trying to get off the ground.

It was ten-thirty and he was yawning. He dropped his head from side to side, stretching his neck and knowing that it was useless going to bed this early. Bitter experience had taught him that no matter how tired he was, he'd lie in bed and think and overthink until he was too wound up to drift off.

Nope. Going to bed before midnight never worked out well for him.

He stood and stretched some more. Maybe some of his colleagues would still be hanging around the bar. A bit of relaxed conversation…a couple of whiskies…

Now, that was the recipe for sleep.

Miranda gently swirled the red wine round and round her glass as she tracked her sexy neighbour's progress across the bar. She'd spied him the instant he'd walked in and their gazes had locked within seconds. He'd smiled at her and she'd smiled back.

And where her heart had been hammering at the sight of him it settled instantly as he started to walk towards her. There was a surrealness about it. But at the same time it felt natural.

It felt a lot like fate.

Which was a big thing for someone who didn't do bar pick-ups. *Who didn't do anything rash or spontaneous.*

Not since she'd been seventeen, anyway.

Yet strangely she didn't seem to be able to stop watching him.

He sat on the stool next to her. 'Couldn't sleep, Miranda Dean?'

That teasing tone of his was so charming and flirty it stole her breath. 'Someone was snoring next door, Patrick Costello,' she murmured.

'Ah…you've been looking me up. Should I be flattered?'

Miranda shook her head. 'Not by that mug shot of you—you look like a criminal.'

He gave a chuckle and it was deep and rich and Miranda found herself wanting to move in even closer. His hair curled in wisps around his ears and at his nape. He was wearing jeans and a casual long-sleeved T-shirt.

'I think that was taken after a particularly heinous nine-hour op,' he said as he motioned to the bartender for a Scotch on the rocks. 'Plus I'm not very photogenic.'

Miranda found that exceedingly difficult to believe. He had that laid-back sex appeal that cameras adored.

'So, Miranda, are you from around here?'

It was Miranda's turn to laugh. 'I'm from Brisbane, yes, but I should let you know right from the start that I am a responsible single mother of one and do not let guys in bars pick me up. I don't even *go* to bars.'

Patrick smiled. *So she was single.* 'Would you believe me if I told you I don't either?'

Miranda shook her head. 'No.' He looked exactly like he hung out in bars. *And never went home alone.* Drinks with colleagues after work. Flirting with the nurses. Smiling that sinful smile at the waitresses.

He gave her a faux wounded sigh. 'Sad but true.'

And somehow she found she believed him. 'So how come you're here now?'

'Can't sleep.' His drink arrived and he held his glass up. 'To insomnia.'

Miranda clinked her glass against his. 'I'll drink to that,' she said, taking a sip of her Shiraz, watching him over the rim as a slug of amber liquid slid down his throat.

Patrick felt the burn all the way down to his stomach. He placed his glass on the bar and turned to face her. Up this close her smoky green eyes and heart-shaped face, free of lines or any kind of adornment, were even more appealing.

He was attracted to her. But more than that, he wanted to *talk* to her.

There was no harm in that, right?

'So where's your daughter tonight? Lola, right?'

He watched her fiddle with the stem of her wine glass.

'Her first sleepover. It's why I've got Pinky. Lola didn't want to take her favourite toy because she's apparently *a big girl now*. But she didn't want Pinky to be home all alone so…I have her.' Her mouth kicked up around the rim of her wine glass as she took a sip. 'Four-year-old logic is hard to explain.'

Patrick knew that intimately. He pulled up his sleeve a little to reveal the dyed macaroni bracelet Ruby had made him a month ago. 'It's okay. I speak four-year-old too.'

Miranda blinked at the lurid colours and before she knew it she was reaching out to touch the made-with-love creation. 'Oh…that's just gorgeous,' she murmured.

It looked so sexy against the dark hairs of his wrist and she was reminded of how she'd admired his broad palm when he had held Lola's miniature pink teddy bear.

Patrick cleared his throat as her light touch had an alarming effect on the artery that pulsed nearby. 'The matching necklace had an unfortunate run in with the shower. Luckily Ruby understood.'

Miranda laughed, looking up from his wrist. His eyes were browny-gold, like autumn leaves amidst his olive complexion and they were staring right at her. She realised she was still touching him and quickly withdrew her hand, her cheeks growing warm.

'Sorry…'

Patrick shook his head, liking how easily she blushed. 'Don't be.'

Miranda felt the breath in her throat grow thick as their gazes locked. 'It's very sweet of you to wear it.'

Patrick shrugged. 'I'm a sweet guy.'

Miranda blinked, breaking the spell. Sweet was not how she would describe him. Sexy, charismatic, masculine. Sweet was too…passive for him.

She took a sip of her wine. 'So…Ruby…that's your daughter?'

Patrick nodded, grateful to Miranda for pulling them back from the edge. He barely knew her yet there was something very hypnotic about her. She was sitting in a bar at close to midnight in jeans, sneakers and a navy V-neck sweater—like Cinderella after the ball. She wasn't loud or effusive like the table full of women over near the window. She wasn't flashing a lot of skin or leaning in close and flirting.

If anything, there was a reserve about her that was intriguing. On the one hand she blushed like a girl but on the other she sat with quiet dignity of a woman well beyond her years.

'Yes.' He smiled when he realised she was waiting for an answer. 'She's five in January.'

'Oh. Lola's five then too.'

Patrick raised his glass to her. 'A good year for babies, obviously.'

He pulled out his wallet and showed Miranda a picture he'd snapped a couple of weeks ago as Ruby had been running around the yard, trying to catch bubbles.

Miranda smiled at the laughing, rosy-cheeked redhead. 'Cute. I can see why you called her Ruby. Does she take after her mother?'

Patrick nodded, caught up for a moment in those first few seconds his daughter had come into the world. 'She has Katie's hair.'

'Katie's your wife?' Miranda asked casually, suddenly afraid to hear the answer. When he shook his head the need to clarify drove her to ask, 'You're not married?'

Patrick looked down at his bare left hand, absently stroking the place where his wedding band, gone for almost three years now, had sat. 'Not any more.'

Miranda, conscious of the occasional brush of his arm and the heat radiating from his thigh to hers, almost sagged against him in relief. She may not be experienced at picking up men in bars and it certainly hadn't been her intention when she'd come to the symposium but she was pretty sure there was an undercurrent between them.

An undercurrent she probably would never have explored under normal circumstances. But Lola was at a sleepover and, thanks to the generosity of her grandmother, she was staying the night at a swanky hotel.

Also, she was extraordinarily attracted to Patrick Costello. And if she wasn't very much mistaken, the feeling was mutual.

This wasn't some seventeen-year-old-girl crush. This was all grown up. And she wanted it. Her pulse tripped at the thought of doing something a little reckless for a change.

She drained the remnants of her glass. Maybe she could have one crazy night?

'Would you like another wine?' he asked.

Miranda met his gaze, felt it rove over her face and settle on her mouth. She'd been a single mother since she was seventeen. She wasn't up on the rules of this situation but the part of her that was female, that responded to his maleness, knew that another wine implied much more than just a second glass.

If she was sensible, she'd walk away right now.

But she was so tired of always being sensible.

She lifted her chin and looked straight into his golden-brown eyes. 'Yes, please.'

They stayed in the bar for another hour talking about their kids and Miranda couldn't remember the last time she'd laughed so hard. Patrick regaled her with funny anecdotes about Ruby's lisp and she told him about Bud, Lola's goldfish, who regularly died, usually just after Lola went to bed, and was reincarnated the next morning thanks to the local pet shop.

'I'm not joking,' Miranda said as his deep laugh drew her closer and closer. 'I have Kevin from the Pet Connection on speed dial.'

By tacit agreement neither of them strayed into personal territory about their circumstances but she did gather that Ruby was with him full time and his ex-wife didn't seem to be around. Also that he had permanent live-in help, which sounded like bliss to Miranda. Her grand-mother was wonderful but she was getting on and Miranda had been so gung-ho proving she could raise her child by herself that she hadn't leaned on anyone more than had been absolutely nec-essary.

But for all their chatter, Miranda had the strang-est feeling that she and Patrick were just marking time. There'd been a sense of inevitability to the night since he'd walked into the bar and it tugged more insistently as the minutes ticked by. But she liked it that he wasn't rushing her back to his room. It felt kind of old-fashioned—in a modern way—and gave him another layer of sexy.

But her yawn at somewhere past midnight spoiled the build-up. 'Sorry,' she apologised, cov-ering her mouth. 'I'm normally passed out cold by nine o'clock.'

He groaned. 'I envy you. I feel like I haven't had a decent sleep since Ruby came along.'

Patrick had enjoyed talking with her. He liked her entertaining stories and easy laugh. He liked how relaxed he felt. He liked how she hadn't out-wardly flirted but he still knew she was into him. He also liked it that any other woman would have jumped in and said *'I can help you with your sleep situation'* but Miranda had just smiled at him.

'Shall we go?' he asked, his voice surprisingly husky.

Miranda nodded. 'Yes.'

They didn't talk as they walked through the bar and across the lobby. They didn't exchange a word as they waited for the lift. Or even inside the lift. Although Patrick leaned on the opposite wall and didn't take his eyes off her for a second. Miranda's belly went into freefall but she held his gaze, anticipation pumping her heart rate higher.

The lift doors opened and he said, 'Yours or mine?' as he ushered her out.

'Mine,' she replied.

She knew zip about one-night stands but she'd heard enough staffroom chatter from other nurses to know she really did not want to be the one doing the walk of shame in the morning.

Patrick stopped outside the door and turned to her. 'Key?'

Miranda reached into her back pocket, slid the piece of plastic out and handed it over. He went to take it but, suddenly nervous, Miranda didn't let go for a moment. He raised an eyebrow. 'You okay?'

The question was low and slid into all the places that were suddenly reminding her how good it felt to be touched. 'I don't…usually do this,' she murmured.

Patrick smiled. 'I figured.' He watched her looking at the door, obviously torn. 'Would it help to know that I don't either?'

Miranda smiled. 'Yes.'

'We don't have to do this, Miranda.'

She blinked at him, searching his face for signs of disingenuousness. Relief flooded through her when she found none. Patrick looked like he was perfectly willing to say goodnight and leave things as they were.

And he'd be gone tomorrow and she'd never see him again.

But she'd always wonder.

She smiled at him, dropping her hand from the key. 'I want to.'

Patrick kept his arm in place, the key still extended in her direction. 'Are you sure, Miranda? Really, really sure?'

She grinned at him. She'd never been surer of anything. 'Open the damn door, Patrick.'

He grinned back then turned towards the door, swiping the card through and hearing the click as the lights turned green. He pushed the door open and said, 'Ladies first.'

Patrick's gut clenched as she brushed past him on the way in, his pulse picking up in anticipation. The door closed behind him and then it was just him and her in the darkened alcove and she was standing there looking at him with possession in her eyes. His groin throbbed in response.

He walked two paces until their bodies were almost touching. She smelled like soap and Shiraz and the combination was intoxicating. He dipped his head to capture her mouth, to savour her taste and to slowly explore her mouth, her neck.

But a little whimper from somewhere at the back of her throat was his undoing and he was deepening the kiss, and her arms were twining around his neck and pulling them together, and before he knew it he'd pushed her up against the wall and they were both breathing hard.

Her hands found the hem of his shirt and it was suddenly gone. Her shirt followed. As did her bra. And as her nipples ruched beneath the pads of his thumbs, his zip was tugged down and her hand was finding its way inside.

He tore his mouth from hers and bit down on a groan. 'Bed,' he said, swinging her up in his arms, kissing her ravaged mouth again as he strode in the general direction, stopped at the mini-bar and panted, 'condoms,' satisfied when she snagged the pack of three that sat propped next to the salted nuts, barely breaking contact.

In four more strides he'd reached the bed and Patrick threw her on the mattress grateful that she'd thought to leave on one of the subdued down lights so he could see her breasts jiggle enticingly.

She was bare to her waist and breathing hard, her hair was spread out in a wild tangle on the white sheets around her.

Three condoms were never going to be enough.

CHAPTER TWO

February

THE LOCKER ROOM was unusually empty for this time of the morning as Miranda climbed into her scrubs. The novelty of scoring a job in the operating theatres at St Benedict's had still not worn off and she inhaled the fresh, clean smell of the shirt as she pulled it down over her head like it was the latest from Versace.

The last few months had been a steep learning curve and she was excited today to be starting her anaesthetics rotation. This was where she was hoping to specialise eventually. Scrubbing in on operations and being a surgeon's right hand was all well and good but she missed the patient contact. At least anaesthetics gave her an opportunity to talk to the people undergoing surgery, even if they were worried and anxious.

Miranda shoved her socked feet into the theatre clogs she'd been issued and grabbed a paper cap from the stash in her locker. She tied it at the back of her head, pleased that she'd decided to cut her hair short rather than have to manage long hair in a theatre cap all day.

The door burst open and two of the more experienced scrub nurses entered, filling the silence. 'I tell you he's hot,' Lilly Martin said. 'The man wears pink scrubs, *pink,* for crying out loud and still manages to look like a sex god.'

'Isn't he married?' Denise Grady queried, nodding at Miranda as she went past.

'Ah, but there's married, then there's *married,* isn't that right, Miranda?'

Miranda was a little intimidated by Lilly's brashness. She'd learned a lot about being a scrub nurse under Lilly's tutelage but she was uncomfortable around the other woman's forceful personality. Lilly was only a couple of years older than her but Miranda felt like a gauche seventeen-year-old again in comparison.

'I wouldn't know,' she murmured, not wanting to get into a debate with Lilly, who could be very opinionated. Married *was* married as far as she was concerned. *No qualifiers*. It certainly made people off limits in her books.

Not that she spent all her spare time on the prowl, as Lilly seemed to do. Or even had any spare time. Between shift work and a five-year-old, her hours were well and truly occupied.

Except for that one night.

Her mind drifted to Patrick. A very naked Patrick sprawled in her hotel bed, smiling that satisfied smile. Her cheeks warmed and her stomach rolled over. It had been everything she could ever have hoped for—she had no regrets.

'Edna said she'd be in Theatre one when you're done here,' Lilly said, breaking into her delicious thoughts of a truly wonderful morning glory.

'Oh, right.' Miranda gave herself a mental shake, dragging her brain back to the present. 'Thanks.'

She left Lilly and Denise to their gossip session and headed down the long corridor that separated the theatres on one side from the storerooms, staffrooms and offices on the other. St Benny's had eight operating theatres. Six were running today with the morning procedures all about to get under way.

Goose-bumps pricked her bare arms as the frigid environment caused her to shiver. The theatres seemed to have only two temperatures— freezing cold or, if you were scrubbed and gowned under huge operating lights, boiling hot.

Miranda pushed open the swing doors to theatre one's anaesthetic room. Edna, an ex-army nurse, who had been at St Benny's since Eve had been a child, looked up from a trolley and smiled.

'Miranda, my dear, how are you?'

Miranda smiled. 'I'm fine, thanks.'

Edna was the stereotypical mother figure, round and jolly and protective of her brood of new grads, though it had taken Miranda only a few days to figure out that you could take the woman out of the army but not the army out of the woman. Edna ran whichever theatre she was in charge of like a military operation and did not suffer fools gladly.

Including prima donna surgeons.

'Right.' Edna smiled. 'Let's get started. All this week will be spent familiarising yourself with machinery and drugs *and* some theory,' she said, waving a thick booklet in the air, 'then you'll have a couple of shifts teamed up with a mentor and next week you'll be on your own. How does that sound?'

'Terrifying?' Miranda admitted.

Edna chuckled. 'You'll be fine, dear. Just remember, if in doubt, ask. The anaesthetists won't bite.'

Miranda nodded. Sage advice she fully intended to take.

The anaesthetists at Benny's were experienced and very open to teaching and formed part of the great team atmosphere Miranda loved so much. Patients always raved about their surgeons and took the poor old anaesthetist for granted. If only they understood it was the anaesthetists who had the most important job—they were the ones keeping the patients alive during the operation!

Miranda absently hoped that the new guy—*the god in pink scrubs*—was also a team player. It only took one rotten apple to make a workplace insufferable.

Half an hour into her orientation the swing doors opened and Genevieve Cowan, the director of anaesthetics, entered, chatting to a man in pink scrubs.

A very familiar man in pink scrubs.

Patrick?

Even with his hair hidden by his blue theatre cap, she recognised him instantly. And even if she'd been suddenly blinded her traitorous cells would have whispered his presence to her anyway. Every single oxygen molecule inside Miranda's lungs seemed to burst in unison and for a moment she struggled to catch her breath.

'This is Edna,' Genevieve was saying. 'I don't think you've met her yet.'

Miranda watched as Patrick extended his hand and shook Edna's saying, 'Nice to meet you.'

Patrick was the sex god in pink scrubs? It was all falling into place now. And then a truly horrifying thought fell into place.

He was married?

'Edna has been here for ever and she knows where every single thing in this place lives. If you need something, she's the woman for the job.'

Miranda barely heard Genevieve as her gaze flew to Patrick's left hand. The macaroni bracelet that had adorned his wrist six months ago was gone. But a plain gold band on his ring finger was out and proud.

'She's also,' Genevieve continued, unaware of

Miranda's complete turmoil, 'the best anaesthetic nurse you'll ever meet.'

Married.

He was married.

She'd slept with a married man.

Her throat constricted. Nausea threatened.

Edna folded her arms across her ample bosom. 'Flattery will get you everywhere, Dr Cowan.'

And then she laughed her giant honking laugh, yanking Miranda out of her escalating panic just in time to hear her own introduction.

'And this is Miranda Dean,' Genevieve said. 'She's new to our team here at Benny's and I believe this is her first day on anaesthetic rotation?'

Miranda looked at the floor, wishing it would swallow her whole, desperate to disappear into thin air. She wanted to go. To run. To run and not stop. To never have to face Patrick and what they'd done.

What *she'd* done.

Patrick frowned at the familiar name as his gaze swung towards the other occupant of the room, who seemed to be finding the floor utterly fascinating. Miranda Dean?

His Miranda Dean?

The woman he'd thought about every day, dreamed about every night for the last six months?

Surely not?

'Miranda?'

He watched as the woman slowly raised her head to look at him. Smoky green eyes peered out from a familiar heart-shaped face and he smiled as his body took a walk down memory lane, reacting to her presence on a purely primitive level.

She didn't smile back.

'Patrick,' she acknowledged through stiff lips, every letter sticking in her toast-dry throat.

'You two know each other?' Genevieve asked.

Patrick felt his gut tighten at Miranda's less-than-enthusiastic welcome. 'Yes,' he said. 'We met at the medical symposium in September.'

'Excellent.' Edna beamed. 'It's always nice to see a familiar face when you're new.'

Patrick wasn't sure Miranda agreed. Why on earth did she look so mortified? He knew what had happened between them had been out of character for her but there was no need to look so guilty about it.

They were both adults, for crying out loud.

'Listen, Miranda, Patrick, do you mind if I snaffle Edna while I've got her?' Geneveive asked. She turned to Edna. 'I need to make some changes to tomorrow's theatre five list.'

Edna nodded. 'Sure. Come to the office.' She looked at Miranda. 'I shouldn't be too long.'

Neither of them waited for approval from Miranda and Patrick and within seconds they were alone.

Patrick frowned at her as Miranda continued to look at him like he'd given her a particularly nasty disease. 'I gather you're not too thrilled to see me?' he started tentatively.

Miranda snorted, galled at his calmness. 'You could say that.'

Okay…she was obviously annoyed about something. 'Look, if you're worried I'll…talk about what happened with us, there's really no need. I don't kiss and tell.'

Miranda folded her arms across her chest. 'How very magnanimous of you.'

Patrick's extremities almost contracted frostbite from the ice in her tone. 'I'm sorry.' He shook his head. 'I don't understand. Did you expect me to call you?'

That hadn't been the impression he'd been left with that morning. True, they hadn't had *the talk* but there'd been something about their goodbye that had been final.

Sure, in another time and place, if his circumstances had been different, he'd have followed up but they'd both lived in different cities and had had obligations to their families.

He'd been pretty sure she'd known it too.

'I expected you to not *be married!*' she snarled.

For a second or two Patrick was very confused then he looked down at his wedding ring.

Damn it! He was so unused to wearing it he'd forgotten he'd put it back on.

'Oh, no.' He shook his head emphatically. 'No, no, no. This is not what it looks like,' he hastened to assure her.

Miranda was so angry she could barely see straight. *He'd lied to her.* To get her into bed. She'd specifically asked him the question and he'd denied it. And like some stupid young affection-starved fool she'd believed him. 'So you aren't married?' she demanded.

Patrick sighed. 'Well...*technically* I am, but—'

'Oh, God,' Miranda wailed, shutting her eyes, hoping she could block him and what had happened out. It had been the most amazing night of her life and now it had been totally sullied by his lies. 'I don't believe this.'

'Look,' Patrick said, taking a step towards her as she opened her eyes.

Miranda stabbed her finger in the air towards him. 'Stay right there,' she hissed. 'Do not come *any* closer.'

Patrick stopped, holding his hands up in surrender. He was pleased that the daggers in her eyes were purely metaphorical because she looked like she could do damage with a sharp pointy weapon right about now. 'Let me explain.'

Miranda laughed at his audacity. 'Oh, okay, fine.' She folded her arms again. 'Go ahead. Explain to me how you're married but not really and how it doesn't make you *and me* lying, cheating, despicable human beings?'

Patrick heard the tap, tap, tap of her clog against the hard floor. Saw the determined little tilt to her chin. God, he couldn't go into it all here. It was a life *he* still found difficult to believe he was living. 'Not here, Miranda. It's…complicated.'

Miranda nodded. She knew all about complicated relationships. Growing up an illegitimate child of the *other woman,* she was intimately acquainted with complicated.

'Yeah,' she said, 'the married ones always say that.'

Patrick frowned. *What on earth did that mean?* 'Why don't we get coffee or lunch together today? I can explain, Miranda.'

Miranda shook her head. It didn't matter. What was done was done. And having lunch, coffee or any contact with this man simply wasn't on the table.

Thankfully Edna and Geneveive bustled back through the door and she was spared from any further conversation.

Miranda rushed to the school later that afternoon. Flexibility of hours at St Benny's had been one of the draw cards, along with its closeness to home, but it was unavoidable that Lola was going to need to use the after-school care facilities from time to time—her grandmother already did too much without adding to her burden of care. Luckily Lola was a social little girl who made friends easily.

Today, though, not even thoughts of her daughter could elicit a smile as she went over and over her conversation with Patrick, her head thumping a little harder each time. Thankfully she'd seen very little of him for the remainder of the shift and then only at a distance. Twice it had looked like he was going to approach her and she wasn't too proud to admit she'd deliberately walked in the other direction.

A squall of emotions had taken up residence in her belly and she didn't want him near her until she'd thought them through.

It was hard to get her head around the startling implications of his beringed presence and its impact on her sense of self. Dressed in pink scrubs, he had indeed looked like the sex god he'd been declared but having grown up the casualty of infidelity Miranda hadn't allowed his devastating sexual attraction to be a factor.

She'd formed very early opinions of the sanctity of marriage that she had staunchly lived by. Married men were simply off limits.

No exceptions.

No grey areas.

And yet she'd slept with one. The mere thought kicked up the squall in her stomach another notch.

Sure, he'd said he could explain and she had no doubt there was some tale of woe about being separated, about how his wife didn't understand him or how they had an open marriage.

She was sure there was some easy patter about the *technicality* of his marriage.

But she didn't want to hear any of it.

What they'd done had been unforgiveable. What *he'd* done had been unforgiveable. And after eight hours of stewing over it she was even more annoyed now than she had been initially. White-hot anger boiled in her belly.

Add to that disgust, abhorrence and humiliation and she had a headache the size of Australia banging away at her frontal lobe.

Frankly, she couldn't wait to go home and have a shower and wash away the guilt and the stain of her transgression. She'd spent six months fantasising about that night, living every deliciously sexy moment over and over, and he'd dashed it all in one day.

She felt dirty. She felt used.
She felt like a fool.
All she wanted to do was get home, have that shower and hug her daughter hard.

Lola gave her one of those big, girly, whole-face grins as she walked into the centre and Miranda felt her headache ease a little. Her heart did its usual squeeze in her chest.

Being a teen mum had been hard and it would never have been a choice she'd have made for herself voluntarily, but her little blonde-ringletted baby girl was simply the best thing that had ever happened to her. Lola filled her heart with joy every day and Miranda couldn't even begin to imagine life without her daughter.

Lola ran across the room in her usual excitable way and threw herself at Miranda's body. 'Mummmmmy!'

Miranda laughed as she clutched her daughter close, kissing her beautiful curls. It was hard to believe that an insane teenage coupling born from rebellion and disaffection had resulted in the perfect little person in front of her. Sleeping with a transient surfer dude only a couple of years older than herself had been a three-week moment of madness but his DNA could not be faulted.

'Come on, darling,' Miranda said, crouching down and accepting an enthusiastic kiss. 'Get your bag. Let's go home.'

'Can my new best friend in the whole world come too? For a tea party? We could have Nan's cupcakes and drink Earl Grey just like real ladies.'

Miranda gave an inward groan as her headache thumped in earnest. The very last thing she wanted to do now was to entertain another child. 'I'd need her mummy's permission, Lols. Let's do it another day, okay? Maybe at the weekend? I'll get her number from the phone tree.'

Lola clasped her hands together as if she was an orphan asking for more food. 'Oh, no, Mummy, pleeeeeease? I love her. I love her. I told her she could come.'

Miranda smiled despite her tiredness and felt her little girl's passionate entreaty worm its way under her skin. 'Lols...'

Lola shifted from foot to foot and clapped. 'I'll go and get her.'

Miranda stood and sagged in resignation. Any

other day she'd have brushed off Lola's sneaky big-eyed plea with a firm *'Not today'* but life had battered her a little too much these last eight hours and children could always spot a weakness.

She turned to ask the teacher for the list of parent phone numbers. She seriously doubted the other mother would say yes—she certainly wouldn't let Lola go to a place she wasn't familiar with and to people she didn't know—but maybe they could set something up for the weekend.

The very last person she expected to see walking through the front door was Patrick.

For a moment she forgot he was a lying, cheating sneak who had put her in a morally untenable position and just rode the surge of undiluted lust that brushed her skin in a crimson flush. Memories of his kiss, of his heat, of his hardness flooded in and muscles deep inside her tightened in recognition.

God, she wanted him again. Wanted to drag him into the little room where she knew they kept the supplies, strip his clothes off and do him against the wall.

This was what happened when a grown woman

lived her life like a nun. *Inappropriate thoughts about men who did not deserve them!*

He gave her a surprised look and her heart thundered as he approached, even his grim smile with that sinful chin cleft seemed somehow devilishly sexy.

'Are you following me?' she demanded. It seemed irrational but the thumping in her head wasn't exactly allowing for clear thought processes. She didn't know what he was doing here but she certainly didn't want to exchange pleasantries with the man.

Or listen to his excuses.

Patrick blinked at her aggressive tone. He knew he had some explaining to do but he was too tired for female histrionics. 'Don't be ridiculous.'

Miranda folded her arms across her chest. 'I told you I did not want to talk to you about... our...stuff and I don't appreciate you trying to push the issue.'

'Look, Miranda.' He ruffled his hair. 'I'm just here to pick up Ruby, that's all.'

It took a few seconds for Miranda to get the import of his words, distracted as she was by the ruffled sexiness of his hair. She frowned but was interrupted by a 'Mummy' and a yank on her jeans. She looked down blankly, pleased for the respite from his weary brown eyes that tugged in places they had no right to be tugging.

Her blonde curly-haired moppet blinked up at her, one skinny arm slung around the neck of a cute little redhead with rosy cheeks and her father's eyes.

'This is Ruby,' she announced. 'My new bestest friend for ever. She has a lipth. Please, Mummy, please can she come over for cupcakes?'

'Pleath, Daddy,' the little redhead added. 'Pleeeeeath.'

Patrick smiled down at his daughter. Ruby tended to be on the quiet side and it was unusual for her to make such a fast friend so it eased his conscience over the move. He looked at Miranda and shrugged. 'I'm okay with it if you are.'

Miranda felt cornered. She was absolutely, one hundred per cent *not* okay with it. But she'd have to choose her words carefully in front of little ears. Somehow *'I'd rather stick a red-hot poker in my eye than have a low-down cheating skunk in my house'* didn't seem appropriate with their audience.

'Pleeeeeath,' Ruby begged, looking up at Miranda. Her two front teeth were missing, something that no doubt exacerbated the lisp.

'It would give us a good chance to talk,' Patrick murmured close to her ear.

'Pleeeeeease, Mummy.'

Miranda took in all three, each in their own way desperate for something from her, and knew when she was defeated. 'Okay,' she acquiesced. 'But only for a short visit. I've got a bit of a headache and tomorrow will be another long day.'

'Yaaaay!' Two little girls squealed and jumped up and down, hugging each other, strands of blonde and red hair intertwining.

'Yay,' said Patrick.

But his voice was lower, edgier, sexier and slid into places he'd already been and *shouldn't* have.

Miranda shivered.

Twenty minutes later the knock on her front door heralded Patrick and Ruby's arrival and Miranda felt the squall inside intensify. The two tablets she'd taken for her headache had started to work but the thump returned with a vengeance as Lola squealed and raced to answer the door.

Miranda looked around her small two-bedroom residence feeling suddenly inadequate. She'd been living above her grandmother's garage since before Lola's birth and although she'd made it into a nice cosy home, it wasn't where she wanted to spend the rest of her life.

Patrick probably lived in a mansion. On the river. With a city view. What would he make of this?

Lola and Ruby ran past her into Lola's bedroom in a blur of blonde and red and left her alone with Patrick standing in the doorway in his business shirt and trousers looking tired and sexy and rumpled, just like he had that night six months ago. Her heart fluttered madly.

'Hi.' He smiled.

Miranda wanted to smile at him too. Say hi back as she walked straight into his arms and gave in to the passion that still burned deep inside despite her animosity. He looked so at home in her doorway it was scary.

She took a breath. 'Come in,' she said. It felt stiff and awkward but that was too bad. 'Would you like a coffee?'

'Sure.'

Patrick pushed off the doorframe. She looked tired and wary and he couldn't blame her but her jeans clung and her T-shirt stretched nicely across breasts he'd dreamed about a little too much, and he was right back there in that hotel room with her.

He followed her across the lounge into the open-plan kitchen, leaning his butt against a bench as she busied herself. 'You've cut your hair,' he said.

Miranda, hyper-aware of him standing behind her, absently touched her nape where her pixie cut now feathered. 'Yes,' she said, her hands shaking as she poured hot water into mugs.

She supposed he had some fancy Italian coffee machine that made double-shot decaf lattes. All she had was instant and an electric jug.

'Mummy, can we have cupcakes now?'

Miranda turned, pleased for the interruption. She nodded at her daughter and Patrick's, looking all Shirley Temple and little orphan Annie. 'It's all set. Help yourselves.' Lola clapped excitedly. 'But remember, it's polite to serve your guest first.'

Lola nodded. 'Come on, Ruby—Mummy and I made a tea party!'

'Come on, Daddy,' Ruby said, tugging on his hand as Lola pulled her towards the table.

He shrugged at Miranda. 'Sorry.'

'It's fine. Go and join them. I'll bring your coffee.'

Miranda wrapped her hands around a mug and thanked the universe for the breathing space. She'd felt his gaze on her neck like a caress and could almost feel his lips brushing there too.

She pulled herself together and fixed the coffees, lecturing herself about the inappropriateness of her thoughts. By the time she walked on spaghetti legs to the exquisitely set table she felt more in control.

'Thanks,' Patrick said, as she put his mug down.

It looked out of place amidst the fancy-looking china that Lola had insisted they use for the impromptu tea party. Her grandmother had bought it for Lola a couple of years ago and though it had been inexpensive, it looked fit for a queen.

'I'm sorry,' she apologised. 'It's all a bit girly.'

Patrick smiled and shook his head. 'I like a tea party as much as the next man,' he declared, and the girls laughed hysterically as he stuck out his pinky and sipped his coffee.

'Your daddy is funny,' Lola said around a mouthful of cake.

Miranda agreed.

And sexy and manly and one hundred per cent at home in an environment that was suffocating in oestrogen. Which only ramped up his own masculinity. He looked so incredibly male amidst the frippery of a girly afternoon tea with the china and the delicate pink cupcakes, she wanted to drag him to her bedroom, rip his shirt open and rediscover every inch of his maleness.

Play a little doctor and nurse.

They made stilted conversation with their daughters for ten minutes before Lola announced they were going to watch some *TV*.

And then there were two.

Miranda stood and started gathering dishes. When Patrick placed a stilling hand on her arm she ignored it, continuing her task with manic speed.

'Miranda,' he said quietly, refusing to remove his hand, refusing to be ignored. 'I need to explain.'

Miranda shook her head. 'No,' she said as she pushed crumbs from one plate onto another. 'No, you don't. Let's just pretend it never happened and move on, okay? I won't mention it, you won't mention it…' she stacked plates one on top of the other and picked them up, turning to leave '…and it'll be fine.'

Patrick applied a little more pressure on her forearm and he felt the weight of her gaze as it moved to his hand, his gold wedding band a reminder of their predicament. 'Miranda, we have to work together,' he said gently. 'I do need to explain. Sit. Please.'

Miranda would rather have enrolled in a medical trial that involved daily root-canal treatment but deep down she knew he was right. They did have to clear the air, for their professional life if nothing else. Or one of them was going to have to leave.

And she was guessing it would have to be the most expendable.

Which would be her.

She sat.

CHAPTER THREE

PATRICK HAD FORMULATED a spiel in his head on the drive to Miranda's. But it didn't seem adequate enough now as she sat stiffly, staring transfixed at the table as if the debris littering the lacy cloth was diamond chips instead of cake crumbs.

Whatever else he said, he knew he had to start with an apology. 'I'm sorry I wasn't one hundred per cent honest with you at the bar that night.'

Miranda didn't take her eyes off the table. 'Well, it's *complicated*, right?'

Patrick sighed. 'It is. It really is.'

Miranda glanced up at the resigned exasperation in his tone. Like he'd known she was going to judge him and there was nothing he could do about it. Except there was.

He could stop sleeping with women other than his wife!

'And because I was just some…bar pick-up…'

even saying the words made her feel sullied '…I wasn't owed the truth?'

He rubbed his hand along his jaw and Miranda could tell he was choosing his words carefully. 'Yes,' he admitted. 'And no.'

Miranda felt her blood pressure skyrocket. *Obviously he wasn't choosing his words carefully enough.* 'I see,' she said, looking back at the table again.

Patrick groaned inwardly at the barriers she was building at a rate of knots. So different from the Miranda of six months ago who, although reserved, had been receptive and aware of their vibe.

A vibe that had roared to life again this morning.

Right at this moment she was so shut down he wondered if she'd ever speak to him again. He was trying to be honest but his situation wasn't typical. 'It's not something I talk about much. *To anyone.* Certainly not…'

Miranda tossed her head and glared at him. 'Women you pick up in bars?'

'It wasn't like that, Miranda.'

'*Of course not,*' she said derisively. 'So what *is*

it like?' she demanded, her voice quiet but loaded with don't-screw-with-me attitude. 'Is she frigid? A shrew? Sexually unavailable? Or maybe she just can't *love you the way you need?*'

Patrick blinked at the rapid-fire choices she'd given him. Her lip had curled at each option, her voice full of derision. If he had to take a guess he'd say Miranda had more than a passing acquaintance with infidelity.

He took a breath. It was understandable that she was angry. He had to accept that.

'My wife…Kate…Katie…went missing when Ruby was six weeks old. I haven't seen her since.'

Miranda had prepared herself for the usual platitudes. Even for the not so usual. But nothing had prepared her for this. She frowned as she tried to wrap her head around what he'd said. 'Missing?'

Patrick nodded. 'I came home from work one evening to an empty house and a screaming baby.'

Miranda let go of the plates with a clatter and without even thinking about her actions reached out to touch his hand. Her anger and disappointment dissolved. What a truly awful thing to happen. 'I'm so…sorry. I didn't realise…'

Patrick shrugged. Her touch felt good and the empathy in her smoky green gaze reached right inside him and squeezed. He'd thought he was over the rawness of that time, a time when his entire life had been turned upside down, but talking to Miranda about it was surprisingly difficult. The worry and the fear and the anger were mixing again in a potent tangible force.

'It's fine. Not really bar-conversation material though…'

Miranda nodded. 'Yes, of course, you're right.'

The facts may not have changed—she had still slept with a married man. But he was right, it was *complicated*. And totally understandable not to have confided in her, a stranger, that night in the bar.

Or at any stage really. How did a person work that into a one-night stand—'Oh, by the way, I'm married but it's okay because she's been missing for five years'?

Perhaps he wasn't such a skunk after all.

She became aware that she was still touching him and withdrew her hand. It felt right to proffer some small gesture of comfort but there was a lot more that needed to be said.

'So…what happened? Is she, Katie…is she…?'

Patrick watched her face as she obviously tried to approach the question with delicacy. 'Dead?' he asked.

Miranda baulked at his blunt delivery and the bleakness in his eyes. Was this what made him look so tired all the time? Did he lie awake every night wondering where she was? Worrying? Grieving for his wife?

'Well…yes.' It had been the question foremost in her mind but she'd hoped to put it more delicately. Along with the hundreds of other questions that crowded inside her waiting to be asked.

'No. She's out there somewhere.' Patrick raked his fingers through his hair. It was hard to admit—his wife, Ruby's mother, was *choosing* to stay away.

That's probably what hurt most.

Miranda caught a glimpse of the pain and suffering he must have gone through reflected in the agitated rake of his fingers. She could see it was hard for him and she put her hand out again, touching his forearm.

'You don't have to talk about this.'

Patrick looked down at her hand and placed his

over the top then smiled at her. 'Yes, I do. Because if I'd slept with you that night and never seen you again, it would have been fine. But here we are. So I need you to know.'

Miranda nodded and withdrew her hand. It felt too intimate and as much as her empathy meter was blinking off the scale, there were still a lot of reasons why getting too close to Patrick was a bad idea.

If anything, he was even more off limits. Getting involved with a man who was hung up on another woman was just plain dumb.

She only needed to look to her mother for a perfect example of that.

'Okay. So what happened?' she asked.

'There was an extensive search for her. It was all over the news…'

Miranda thought back and did vaguely recall something now about a missing mother that she'd obviously absorbed subliminally in her new-mother fog with a colicky baby who rarely slept and while studying for her grade-twelve exams.

'Weren't you…implicated in that?'

Patrick grimaced. 'Initially, yes. Despite the

fact I'd been at work all day for twelve hours with dozens of witnesses.'

Miranda supposed she should have been concerned about that startling piece of information but there was nothing about Patrick that raised her highly developed *run-away-fast* instincts.

She searched her brain for more titbits for a moment then gave up. 'I don't remember what happened after that… Lols was brand new and my life officially sank into a black hole for quite a few months.'

'There was a media storm and some pretty harrowing questioning by the police and then after two weeks Katie contacted her mother. Left a message on her mother's machine. Said she was okay but she didn't want to be a mother any more. Had never wanted it. That she was going away and wasn't coming back.'

Miranda felt the pressure of something hard and hot wedging under her diaphragm. She couldn't begin to imagine the state she would need to have been in to abandon Lola. To never see her again. She shook her head in bewilderment. 'Was there…? Were you having problems?

Do you think she was suffering from post-natal depression?'

Patrick liked how easy it was to talk to Miranda. Just like in the bar that night. Most people were emotional and animated or listened with ghoulish delight but, once again, Miranda was reserved and thoughtful.

'She was only twenty-one when we met. She was in her last year of nursing and doing her prac at the same Sydney hospital where I was an intern. She was this bright, sparkly butterfly. The life and soul of the party, and I was hopelessly smitten. But it was all a façade. She was actually desperately insecure and anxious and she…had some problems with substance abuse. After a few months I began to suspect she was a little bipolar and our relationship had become quite rocky.'

'And then she fell pregnant,' Miranda supplied. She understood only too well what a life-changing event that was.

Patrick nodded, feeling again the highs and lows of that time. The dread, the fear, the excitement.

'She was great at first. On a high, I guess. Happy to clean up her act and get married and excited about being a mother. But by the time Ruby was due she was quite down, very flat. I finally managed to convince her to see her GP, who wanted her to go on some antidepressants but she was adamant she wouldn't take anything while she was pregnant.

'And then in the weeks after the birth she got worse. I tried to get her to see somebody but she refused. When I came home that evening to find she wasn't there, a part of me wasn't surprised. But I never thought she'd just disappear…just go…for good…'

Miranda leaned forward a little in her chair. He was twisting his wedding ring round and round his finger with his thumb, the low strain of emotion in his voice giving her goose-bumps.

'Do you think she had a bit of a…breakdown that day?'

He shrugged. 'I think so, yes. Gwen, our neighbour at the time, said she'd seen Katie leave the house clutching her handbag and looking in a bit of a daze. Katie didn't apparently even acknowledge Gwen when she asked how things were going with the baby.'

Miranda was no mental-health expert but

that didn't sound good to her. 'But she rang her mother and you were off the hook, right?'

He snorted. 'Not immediately. The police, quite rightly, I suppose, were suspicious about the authenticity of the message, so they ran forensic tests comparing it to the welcome message on our answering machine and eventually they cleared me of any suspicion.'

'So…she's never turned up?'

Patrick shook his head. 'No. The police dropped the investigation once they were satisfied she was alive. I've hired several private investigators but it's hard to find someone who doesn't want to be found.'

Miranda's mind crowded with questions, each more urgent than the next. 'Aren't you worried that she may have come to some harm in the intervening years?'

'Yes,' he said. 'But there's occasional activity on her bank account and every once in a while she rings a great-aunt of hers, tells her she's okay and then hangs up.'

Miranda couldn't even begin to comprehend what he must have gone through in the years since Ruby had been born. The wondering. The not knowing. Not to mention having to be mother and father and juggle job and family responsibilities and finances and a hundred other things.

Just like her.

'I can't begin to imagine what you've been through,' she murmured. 'It must have been *so* hard. To have coped with all that as well as trying to be a father.'

The empathy in her gaze was real and washed over him, oozing into all the cracks that had opened up again as he'd talked about Katie's desertion. 'To be honest, it nearly broke me.'

He paused. It was the first time he'd admitted that out loud. He'd spent a lot of years presenting a tough front but it seemed okay to admit the truth to her. To finally admit it to himself even.

'I didn't cope that well for a while. I kind of just…survived. If it hadn't been for Katie's mother helping out I think I might have gone under.'

Miranda nodded. She was glad Patrick had had someone to lean on. How would she have survived without her grandmother's love and support?

'What does Ruby know about it?' she asked. It

was *the* thing as a mother she found most difficult to comprehend—how could Katie have de-
serted her baby?

Patrick dragged himself back from the helpless-
ness of that time, pleased that he now had time
and distance and perspective.

He shrugged. 'I've just tried to be honest. Ruby,
like Katie, does tend to be a bit on the anxious
side so we don't make a big deal out of it. She
knows she has a mummy who loves her but is
too sick to look after her properly so Daddy does
it instead.'

Miranda pursed her lips. 'Ooh. That's good.'

He grimaced. 'Well, it seems to appease her.
For now. What do you tell Lola about her father?'

'Honestly? Lola is far too egocentric to care.
She asked once when she was two why she didn't
have a daddy and I told her that some kids didn't
have daddies, which seemed to satisfy her perfectly. As long as there's Pinky, Bud and cupcakes in the world, she's happy.'

Patrick laughed at Miranda's candid answer. It
was nice to meet a mother who had her daughter's measure. He'd met many a rabid mother
since having a child of his own and it was nice

for once to talk to someone who wasn't blind to everything.

'So where is he? Lola's father?'

Miranda shrugged. 'On a beach somewhere, I guess.'

'You've lost contact?'

'We never really had contact. I grew up near a really great surf beach and he was there for a few weeks, camping with a bunch of friends, on a big trip around Australia. I was seventeen and…a little on the rebellious side…'

'Seventeen?' Horrified, Patrick did the maths in his head. But no matter how many times he did the simple sum he kept getting the same answer. 'Dear God that makes you…'

'Twenty-two.'

'Oh, God.' Patrick buried his head in his hands. He'd slept with a woman *ten* years his junior? How was it possible that Miranda was just a year older than Katie had been when they'd first hooked up? She was so much more mature in a multitude of ways.

'Is that bad?'

He looked up. 'Very, very bad. I figured you were the other end of twenty.'

'Gee, thanks...'

'Sorry.' He grimaced. 'I didn't mean it like that.'

Miranda laughed at his obvious discomfort. 'It's fine. I was a teen mother—it tends to mature you pretty quickly.'

Patrick groaned again. A part of him had been thinking that maybe they could pick up where they'd left off. 'I'm going to hell.'

Miranda leaned in close to him and whispered, 'It's okay. I wasn't a virgin.'

He winced. 'That is so not funny.'

'Oh, come on.' She grinned. 'It is. Just a little.'

Patrick did not return the grin. After Katie, he'd made a personal vow to never get involved with anyone who could still see twenty in their rear-view mirror.

Seriously? How could she only be twenty-two!

'Miranda, if I'd known you were so young I would never have...' Picked you up in a bar and gone back to your hotel room. 'I'm really sorry.'

Miranda supposed she should be annoyed by his sudden abhorrence over what had happened between them but she was amused and curiously touched by his mental self-flagellation.

She feigned a pout. 'So you didn't enjoy your-self?'

Patrick felt the hole he was in get a little deeper as it appeared he was adding insult to injury. 'Oh, God, please,' he said falling over himself to reassure her. 'Don't get me wrong. You were... great... It was...magnificent... I swear I've thought of little else since.'

He saw her face break into another broad grin and stopped his babbling. 'Ah...' He smiled. 'You mock.'

Miranda's belly flopped as his choice of words took her back to that night. 'Sorry, I couldn't help it. Look, it's fine,' she assured him. 'Really. I'm a big girl. And I wanted it as much as you did. But it's good to see a man with some moral fibre. Lola's father could have taken a page out of your book.'

Patrick latched onto the change in topic like a lifeline. 'He didn't want anything to do with Lola?'

'By the time I knew I was pregnant he'd moved on.'

Patrick felt a prickle of unease. 'So he doesn't

know?' How would he feel if Katie hadn't told him about Ruby?

'No. He knows. I rang and told him. But he freaked out and let me know in no uncertain terms that he wasn't going to be framed as the baby daddy by some groupie chick who probably banged every surfer she met.'

Patrick winced. 'Nice.'

Miranda shrugged. 'Yes. It was a bit of a shock. But…what can you do? I just picked myself up and got on with it.'

Patrick was struck by Miranda's poise. And her maturity. She seemed wise beyond her years. *Her paltry twenty-two years.*

He realised he liked her. A lot. And it had nothing to do with the hours he'd spent in her bed— because that he really, really had to delete from his memory banks—and everything to do with her serenity. Her composure. He was drawn to her as a human being, not just as a woman. He'd had the same feeling that night in the bar when they'd been chatting about their daughters, and it was nice to feel it again.

Suddenly it was just as important that she felt the same way about him. That she *liked* him.

That she knew what had happened at the hotel that night wasn't his usual *modus operandi*. He grew more sober as he sought and held her gaze.

'I didn't lie to you that night,' he said. 'I don't often pick up women in hotel bars.'

Miranda laughed at his phrasing. 'Often?' she teased. 'That's not very convincing.'

He laughed along with her at his dubious word choice. 'The occasional one-night stand on my infrequent sojourns from home is about all I can manage these days so saying I *never* do it would be a lie. But I didn't go to the bar looking for it.'

Miranda nodded. She believed him. She remembered the genuine surprise and delight on his face when he'd spotted her. She looked at his hand still cradling his mug.

'So why the wedding ring?'

Patrick removed his hand from the mug and looked down at the band Katie had bought him about a million years ago now and which he hadn't worn since the last time he'd changed hospitals a few years ago. He studied it quietly for a moment or two.

He looked at her. 'It's a quick and easy way to send a signal about my lack of availability in a new working environment without having any awkward conversations. Sooner or later someone's going to realise that I'm *that* Dr Costello and everything will come out as the gossip takes off.'

Miranda nodded. It was sound reasoning, she supposed, but listening to his tale today and watching him finger the ring almost constantly, she had to wonder if there wasn't a little part of him that was still holding out hope that Katie would come home and they could pick up where they'd left off.

Had she been some kind of Katie substitute that night six months ago?

She must have some doubts on her face because he quirked an eyebrow at her and said, 'What?'

Miranda shrugged. 'I guess I'm just wondering if maybe you're…not quite over her.'

Patrick stilled at the suggestion even as the rejection formed on his lips. 'Yes. I am,' he said, his voice quiet but vehement, his gaze seeking and locking with hers. 'And she needn't think she can walk back into our lives at some stage in the future, after turning her back on not just me but on her *child*, and all will be forgiven. I understand that she probably wasn't in her right mind and hadn't been for a while but what she did was unforgiveable and there's no going back from that.'

Miranda flinched at the steely edge to his voice. She was left in no doubt that, no matter how much it had broken him, Patrick had well and truly moved on. Any feelings he may have had for her had well and truly been killed off by Katie's disappearing act.

'Mummy, can Ruby and I play on the swings?'

'And the thee-thaw,' Ruby added.

Miranda dragged her gaze from Patrick's, grateful for the interruption, and she smiled at the adorable lisp that somehow seemed to make Ruby even cuter. 'It's fine by me. Depends on your daddy.'

'Pleath, Daddy?' Ruby fluttered her eyelashes. 'Pleeeeath?'

'They're just down the stairs in the back yard near the garage,' Miranda supplied. 'It's all securely fenced off from the street.'

Patrick nodded his assent. 'But we do need to be going soon,' he added over the din of excitement as the girls squealed in delight then headed for the door.

Quiet descended as the girls tore down the stairs and Miranda was aware that they were now totally alone. And sitting quite close as the intimacy they'd shared settled around them. She could smell the spicy sweetness of his cologne and memories of how it had filled her senses as he'd rocked into her that fateful night washed over her. The urge to lean in closer, to bury her face into his neck, to lift her mouth to his, beat like a jungle drum through her head and she stood abruptly to pick up the dishes.

This was not the bar of some swanky hotel.

'You can join them if you like,' she said as she moved away and headed to the sink. 'I'll just do these then come down too.'

Patrick's heart banged in his chest as he started to breathe again. For a crazy moment he'd been sure she'd been going to kiss him. Which probably made him clinically insane.

Twenty-two. Twenty-two. Twenty-two.

He stood and gathered the rest of the dishes. 'I'll give you a hand.'

'No, really,' she said as she flicked on the hot

tap, squirting too much liquid detergent in as her brain frantically tried to reel in the call of the wild. 'I'm fine.'

Patrick placed his load on the bench beside the sink and picked up a towel that was hanging over the oven door handle. 'A job shared is a job halved.'

He winced at the trite phrase, grateful when she didn't acknowledge it. 'Besides,' he said, reaching for more sane conversation, 'it looks like we can see them quite well from here.'

Miranda plunged her hands into the hot water, trying to ignore the view of his broad chest in her peripheral vision. She looked straight ahead instead through the large window that looked down on the back yard. The girls were on the see-saw, having a grand old time.

'So this is your grandmother's house?' Patrick asked, desperate to stall the growing awareness of her as their arms occasionally brushed.

Miranda nodded. 'Yes, my grandfather built a granny flat over the garage before I was born. They're both from big families in the UK and would often get visitors for extended periods of time. He died years ago but when my mother kicked me out my grandmother took me in.'

Patrick stopped drying. 'Your *mother* kicked you out? Because of Lola?'

Miranda glanced at him. 'Yes. But it's a long, complicated story.'

Patrick locked his gaze with hers. 'Complicated I get.'

She grimaced at the empathy she saw in his eyes. *He most certainly did.* But she really didn't want to get into the still fraught relationship she had with her mother. 'Unfortunately my headache has had all the complications it can take today.'

Patrick frowned as she rolled her shoulders. 'Have you taken something for it?'

'Yes. It's a little better but I don't want to tempt fate.'

'Well, maybe I can help with that,' he murmured. 'Here, let me.' He dropped the towel on the bench and moved to stand behind her, gliding his palms along her neck muscles.

Miranda felt every cell in her body snap to attention as her hands stilled in the sudsy water.

His aroma enveloped her again as the warmth from his body surrounded her.

'Oh, I'm not sure that's such a good idea,' she said huskily, her eyes shutting as his thumbs brushed her nape.

Patrick had a feeling she was right but pressure points had been a bit of specialty of his during his training. 'Strictly professional, I promise.'

Except it didn't feel professional to Miranda as his thumbs sought and found the place where skull met nape and pushed. In fact, it felt so good she almost arched her back and purred as her head flopped into the pressure.

Patrick felt her body go limp and settle against him. 'How's that?' he asked.

Miranda moaned. 'Stupendous,' she murmured. 'Don't stop.'

Patrick would have smiled had not her moan gone straight to his groin and her husky plea not to stop taken on an entirely different connotation as his body reacted with complete disregard for professional boundaries.

His thumbs gently undulated against the pressure points as he tried to master his physical reaction but even the feather of her dark hair against his fingers was a turn-on. She seemed to lean into him more as he kept the pressure up and he swallowed hard, desperately reminding himself she was twenty-two.

'God,' she groaned. 'That feels so good.'

Twenty-two.

'Your fingers are magic,' she muttered a few seconds later.

Twenty-two.

'Mmm,' she sighed in her next breath. 'You should do this for a living.'

Patrick swallowed. Hard. And hoped she couldn't feel the pounding of his heart against her back or, worse, his inappropriate erection rubbing against her jeans. He should stop. He really, really should. But she was so warm and soft and smelled so amazing. Her aroma was weaving around his good sense like the call of a snake charmer and he was enthralled.

She's a woman.

She's attractive.

You want her.

She angled her neck a little, exposing the beautiful curve of it to his line of sight, and the urge to taste her there beat insistently at his short-circuiting impulse control. He'd probably have managed to ignore it had she not squirmed against him a little and sighed his name under her breath.

And then, before he even knew what he was doing, he dropped his head with a soft groan and brushed his lips across the curve where nape met shoulder.

Miranda's eyes opened as the pressure of his mouth registered. Her pulse tripped madly, her breath felt thick and heavy in her throat. She should pull away. Tell him not to do that. Ask him to stop. But her nipples were hard and her breasts ached and heat pooled deep and low and tingled between her legs.

Was it so bad to want to feel this low steady thrum of arousal every now and then? To feel like a woman?

So she didn't tell him to stop. She did the exact opposite, taking her hands out of the water and slipping them behind her, between their bodies, where she could feel the hardness of him pressing into her and she filled her palms with him and squeezed.

Patrick shut his eyes on a hiss as a lightning bolt scorched his groin. 'Miranda,' he moaned against the shell of her ear, the massage forgotten as he smoothed his hands onto her shoulders and urged her round to face him.

Miranda met his lips with the desperation and passion born from six months of hot dreams and heated fantasies. His palm cupped her jaw and she opened her mouth to him with unashamed need. She clung to his shoulders, whimpered his name, ground herself against him. Needing to get closer. Wanting to reacquaint herself with all of him.

And then his phone rang, loud and insistent, and they broke apart like Ruby and Lola had thrown a bucket of cold water over them.

Hell.

Miranda shook her head. What on earth was she thinking?

She turned away, staring blindly out the window as her pulse pounded through her ears and her breath came hard. She vaguely heard him speaking to the caller as Lola and Ruby played and laughed before her, completely oblivious to what had just happened between their parents.

And they were the stakes, right there.

Two little girls.

This was ridiculous. Crazy. Insane.

A moment of madness.

It may have been fine in an anonymous hotel room at an anonymous conference. But not here. Not now.

Neither of them was free to just follow this stupid powerful pull of lust. They both had someone else they had to put first. She'd tried a relationship a few years ago but her divided loyalties had been its death knell.

Plus she and Patrick worked together.

Patrick ended the call. Miranda had her back to him again and he wished he had some time to wrap his head around their situation. But he did know they couldn't do this. He'd resigned himself to passing on relationships years ago and after all that time of guarding his heart he doubted he even knew how to let someone in.

'We can't do this,' he said.

Miranda turned slowly to face him. 'I know.'

'I'm sorry, I shouldn't have...'

Miranda waved his statement away. 'Neither should I.'

'It's just that...the whole single-dad thing makes it really difficult to...'

Miranda nodded vigorously. 'I know. Truly, I do understand. And we also work together...'

Patrick let his gaze roam over her face. Her smoky green eyes were large in her face, her mouth swollen and ravaged from his kisses. He wanted to take three strides and pick up where they'd left off. 'I wish things were different,' he said.

Miranda nodded. 'So do I.' Then she smiled at him and he smiled back. 'I can cope with being just friends if you can.'

Patrick nodded too, although it sounded depressingly unexciting. 'Sure.' He thrust his hands in his pockets just to be safe. But it wasn't enough. 'I think I'd better get going. Thanks for the tea party.'

Miranda watched as he headed for the door, already hating the strained formality. 'Can you send Lola up for me?'

He didn't look back, just said, 'Will do,' and walked out the door.

Miranda leaned heavily against the kitchen bench, her legs suddenly weak and shaky.

Being *just friends* was going to suck.

CHAPTER FOUR

MUCH TO MIRANDA'S surprise, it didn't suck as much as she'd anticipated. It was awkward initially, for sure, but Patrick was easy to get along with and keen to make the transition smooth. A few weeks down the track she doubted if anyone could tell from their interactions that they'd seen each other naked.

And if, from time to time, she caught him looking at her with heat in his gaze or thoughts of him drifted into a swirling carnal abyss as she helped him anaesthetise a patient then she just reached for her big girl pants and got on with it.

She didn't have time for a flirtation. She was trying to juggle a job and be a single mother and frankly she was just too tired by seven o'clock at night to be sociable. She couldn't do dates or sleepovers and there wasn't room in her brain for feeling sexy when it was crowded with mundane things like the materials she was going to need to make Lola an Easter bonnet for the parade and how she needed to buy sprinkles for the next batch of cupcakes.

No doubt about it—it was an exciting life she led.

But feeling two little skinny arms wrapped tightly around her neck or watching those cute little bow lips slack and perfect in slumber made it all worthwhile.

Later, when Lola wasn't so dependent on her, she could think about dating. About herself.

For now she had one amazing night to get her through.

Patrick checked his watch and drummed his fingers on his thigh as the surgeon uttered a low expletive, despite Edna's disapproving frown. The bowel resection had not been going according to plan, with a lot of bleeding, and everyone was starting to get a little tense.

He kept an eye on the blood pressure of his fifty-eight-year-old patient, Ron. Thanks to a large amount of blood products it was currently being maintained at a reasonable level but it was still too unstable for his liking. There was more cross-matched product available and he had an inkling that Ron was going to need it before the surgery was through.

He looked at his watch again. The operation should have been finished an hour ago. He was going to be late for Ruby. Normally he'd just text Helen to pick up her granddaughter, as she did three afternoons a week anyway, but she was having a rare day off, finally making some new friends after their interstate move, and he didn't want to yank her away from that.

The move had been huge for her too. He'd expected resistance initially but Helen had surprised him with her quick compliance. She'd understood his need to move on, to try and start afresh somewhere else, and Patrick had been thrilled when she'd agreed to come with them.

Some people thought it was strange that he lived with his mother-in-law but they'd always got on well and he couldn't have coped without her these last years—she'd simply been a godsend. And being close to Ruby had helped temper Helen's grief over her daughter's desertion and continuing absence.

Having Helen as live-in help was win-win for both of them.

'I'm knocking off. Denise is taking over—she'll be in shortly.'

Yanked out of his reverie by a voice he thought about a little too much, he looked up into a pair of gorgeous smoky green eyes. The mask hiding the rest of her face only served to emphasise them further.

She was smiling at him. It was right there in her gaze.

He liked her smile. He had the strangest urge to rip the mask off so he could see it. But given Edna's presence and her uncanny knack of knowing when anyone broke the rules, he didn't want to be chastised for spreading respiratory bacteria all over her theatre.

'Could I beg a favour?' he murmured, keeping his voice low. He doubted their conversation could be heard above the surgeons talking to each other, trying to troubleshoot as a team, but he wasn't taking any chances. They'd done a good job of keeping up a professional front and he didn't want to ruin it now.

Miranda nodded, taking the stool beside his

and rolling it a little closer, dropping her ear close to his masked mouth.

'Helen has something on today. Could you pick up Ruby for me and I'll swing by your place after I'm done here? I'm hoping it won't be too much longer.'

'Sure,' she said quietly in return.

It made sense to pick Ruby up and Miranda was pleased to be able to help. She, better than anyone, understood how difficult things could be when the unexpected happened. It didn't matter sometimes how ordered you thought you had your life, when things like this cropped up, the best-laid plans were cast asunder.

'In fact, why doesn't she just stay the night?' she suggested, keeping her voice low. 'Lols has been on at me for the last month about them having a sleepover and it's Friday so no school tomorrow.'

Patrick hesitated. It would certainly help out but Ruby had never been on a sleepover before and he'd be lying if he didn't admit to a level of anxiety over that. Ruby wasn't as gregarious as Lola and with everything that had happened he'd been a little over-protective of her. But, then, she had been nagging him about it too so she was obviously ready.

Even if he wasn't.

Not to mention that it was on the tip of his tongue to ask if the invitation extended to him. A sleepover with Miranda sounded like bliss to him.

'That would be great, thanks,' he said, ignoring the little fantasy and focusing intently on the monitor. 'I'll drop in to say goodnight to her on my way home if that's okay. Actually, I could stop off at home and bring some clothes, too.'

Miranda felt her heart rate pick up a notch. Patrick. Back in her home. She hadn't been able to wash the dishes for a month without reliving that kiss. 'You can but she can always wear something of Lola's.'

Keeping his eye on the screen and the blood pressure, which was starting to fall again, Patrick nodded. 'Okay, I'll wait and see what time I get away from here.'

'No worries. Catch you later,' she said.

'Can you get Denise to get another bag of O-neg?' he asked, louder this time, as Miranda stood.

'Sure thing,' she agreed, also louder, before turning and walking away.

Patrick knocked on the door at quarter to eight. 'You just missed her,' Miranda announced. 'They're both fast asleep after their exciting afternoon.'

Patrick sagged against the doorway. 'Sorry. The case went from bad to worse.'

He'd been keeping her updated via text so she hadn't been concerned. 'It's okay. I told Ruby that you would get here and that you were coming especially to give her a goodnight kiss even if she was asleep.'

Patrick shot her a grateful smile for covering for him. 'Thanks.'

Miranda gripped the door handle tight as his chin cleft winked at her. The top buttons on his business shirt were undone, his sleeves were rolled up, his hair a mixture of theatre-hat flat and finger-combed messy. Black stubble peppered his olive jaw.

He looked tired, harried, harassed.

And so damn sexy her toes were curling. It was the lift all over again.

'You owe me,' she said.

It was futile to be so provocative when they'd agreed to not go there but he seemed to bring out her inner vixen. The one she'd never realised was lurking inside her before she'd met him.

The husky edge to Miranda's loaded comment put Patrick's libido on high alert. She looked so cute in her jeans and T, her feet bare, her toenails painted fairy-floss pink. Her pixie cut framed her face and exposed her neck and a hundred ways of how he could pay his debt to her buzzed through his bloodstream.

He swallowed. 'You know it.'

They didn't say or do anything for a moment and Miranda balanced on a precipice of anticipation, swaying on the edge for long seconds. And then she came to her senses.

Step away from the tired, sexy man.

'Anyway,' she said, falling back from the doorway as she cleared her throat, 'come in. The room's through there if you want to do the honours.'

Patrick, his gaze not leaving hers, took a moment to pull himself together. Reaching for her would be bad so he stuck his hands in his pockets and strode inside, only breaking eye contact as he passed her. By the time he got to the bedroom he was reasonably under control again. And then, of course, his heart melted at the sight of a sleeping Ruby.

The girls were in a double bed that looked suspiciously like it might be Miranda's, given the rather grown-up decor. He shuffled around to Ruby's side and sat down gently. She looked so peaceful and his heart contracted at how anxious she could get from time to time. He wanted her to be happy and well adjusted, which was the main reason for their fresh beginning.

And with Lola's easy friendship she seemed to have taken to it like a duck to water.

He leaned in and kissed her forehead gently. 'I love you Ruby-loo,' he whispered.

Ruby, never the heaviest of sleepers, stirred, her eyelashes fluttering open. 'Daddy...' She smiled sleepily. 'You came.'

Patrick smiled down at her. 'Of course,' he murmured, not wanting to wake Lola. 'I said I would and I always will, Ruby-loo. Promise.'

Although Ruby wasn't yet aware of the events that had shaped all their lives since her birth, she'd obviously picked up on the stress and ten-sion over the years and he knew that manifested itself in her penchant for clinginess.

She was a sensitive child. Like her mother.

Miranda stood in the doorway, listening, her heart beating a firm, steady tattoo in her chest. She knew she probably shouldn't be intruding but she'd been drawn to the room like the prover-bial moth to flame. And seeing Patrick with his daughter, she knew why. Why would she want to miss this? He was sweet and tender and loving.

And, God help her, that was sexy too.

Must *everything* the man did be sexy?

'I like staying with Miwwy, Daddy, sheth fun.'

Patrick, oblivious to Miranda's presence, smiled. He couldn't agree more. Although the fun he had in mind was slightly more adult. 'Yes, she is.' He pushed Ruby's hair off her forehead and dropped another kiss there. 'Now back to sleep. I'll come and pick you up in the morning.'

'You won't be lonely, will you, Daddy?'

Patrick looked into her earnest little face, saw the shine of worry in her eyes. 'Nope. I'm going straight to sleep. No time to get lonely.'

Ruby's face brightened. 'You could thay here. Lola won't mind if you thleep with uth.'

Patrick chuckled quietly. He knew the harm one set of kiddy feet could do to a grown man—he didn't want to experience two sets. And, frankly, if he was staying here, he knew who he'd rather share a bed with. 'It wouldn't be a sleepover if I was here,' he pointed out.

Ruby thought about it for a moment. 'Hmm. Okay, Daddy. You can go home.'

He grinned. 'Okay, then.' He kissed her cheek. 'Night-night, Ruby-loo.'

'Night-night, Daddyoo.'

Patrick eased off the bed as Ruby turned on her side. He stilled as Lola muttered something in her sleep and turned too. He held his breath, hoping she would settle and that he and Ruby hadn't woken her. When she slumbered on he let out his breath and headed towards the door.

Two smoky green eyes and a wistful smile met him and he faltered a little as awareness arced between them. He returned her smile and willed his legs to keep working. 'Sorry,' he whispered, as he drew level with her. 'I hope I didn't disturb Lola.'

Miranda liked how he whispered, all low and husky. It reminded her of the things he'd whispered in her ear that night at the hotel and her skin broke out in goose-bumps, her nipples tightening.

'Don't worry,' she said as she rubbed her arms and led them out of her bedroom. He'd looked too at home in her room, sitting on her mattress, oozing all that weary sexiness over her bed. 'She has her father's ability to sleep like a log. Trying to get her out of bed in the morning is always a challenge.'

Patrick was surprised by the urge to slide his hand onto her shoulder as she walked slightly in front of him. Just to touch her. To stay connected. The level of comfort he already felt in her company was startling.

'Is she very like him?' he asked, to divert such a ridiculous urge.

Miranda turned to face him. 'Physically, yes. She has blonde curls and his eyes and his confident little strut. Not to mention his chilled personality and his coma-like sleeping ability. But...' she shrugged '...I only knew him for three weeks.'

He nodded. 'Was Ruby…okay? She can be a little…anxious sometimes.'

'She seemed fine.'

He rubbed a hand over his jaw. 'It's my fault, I fear. There's been a lot of drama in her young life and I've tried to shield her from it but I've probably gone a little overboard.'

The scrape of his stubble was loud in the silence that lay between them. It was erotic, seductive, evocative. Filling her head with flashbacks. That, combined with his concern for Ruby, was pretty irresistible and she found herself reaching out, placing her hand on his forearm in a gesture of comfort.

Their gazes locked. 'Being a single parent isn't easy. You do the best you can with what you have.'

Patrick's head pounded with the beat of his pulse. Her touch wasn't meant to be sexual but her gaze was smoky with desire and he could feel the pull between them that only sheer willpower was keeping leashed.

'Ain't that the truth,' he murmured.

Miranda could barely breathe as the incendiary atmosphere sucked away all the oxygen. This had to stop or they were going to end up having sex right here and now on the carpet.

She dropped her hand—much more difficult than she'd thought. 'I have some spaghetti Bolognese left over if you're hungry.'

Patrick breathed again as the screeching anticipation receded. 'That might not be such a good idea,' he said, acknowledging their simmering chemistry.

'Probably not.'

'But I am hungry,' he said. His gaze dropped to her mouth. 'Starving, actually.' His eyes returned to capture hers again. 'And something smells good.'

Miranda swallowed. It was difficult enough to ignore the heat between them without him stoking it further. 'Take a seat. I'll dish some up.'

Her five-minute break from him didn't feel like much of a reprieve. In a flat where the living and kitchen area was essentially all in the one open-plan room, she couldn't really hide and she was conscious of him watching her.

But it did give her a chance to collect herself a little and by the time she handed him his plate she was feeling on a more even keel.

'Thanks,' Patrick said as aromas of garlic and basil embraced him, and he dug his fork straight in. He shut his eyes as the flavours mixed on his palate and his tastebuds went into rapture. At least something tonight was going to leave here satisfied.

'This is good,' he said, opening his eyes to find her sitting in the chair opposite.

Miranda laughed. 'Thank you. It's my nan's recipe.'

'Didn't you say she's English?'

'She is. But her specialty is Italian cooking. I think there may have been a fling with an Italian boy back in the days before my grandfather.'

Miranda had always figured that was why her grandmother had been so supportive of her—she understood brash teenage impulsiveness.

'Ah.' He smiled as he took another mouthful. 'Bravo to that.' He ate some more and helped himself to the fresh crusty bread on the side of his plate.

He finished off his serving and smiled at Miranda, who had watched him eat. 'There's this little Italian restaurant near where we lived in Sydney,' he said. 'Run by three generations of

Antonios. This meal is as good as any I've had there.'

Miranda blushed at the compliment. 'I'll tell my grandmother you approve.'

Her blush was distracting and he smiled at her. 'And I'll let Antonio know he has competition.' As soon as he said it he realised his mistake. He was hardly likely to bump into any of the Antonios nearly a thousand kilometres from their home. He sobered a little. 'Or maybe not.'

Miranda sobered as well. 'You miss home? Sydney?'

'No.' He shook his head. 'I don't. I really don't.'

Miranda cocked an eyebrow. 'You could have fooled me.'

Patrick gave a grudging chuckle. 'Well, I miss Antonio's cooking but…there's a lot of memories there, good and bad. I felt like they were holding me back and it was time to move forward. To start afresh.'

'A change can be good,' she said.

He nodded. 'It felt like my life was in a holding pattern in Sydney. Always wondering at the back of my mind if Katie was just going to waltz back into our lives again. And somehow giving her permission to do so by staying there. Conscious of everyone watching my every step. Of the rumours and the gossip and the judgment.'

'That's no way to live your life,' she murmured.

'No.' He smiled at her. 'I wanted to be free of that kind of speculation. I want Ruby to be free of it. I wanted to start living my life again instead of living it in waiting, like everyone around me seemed to expect.'

'Well, that's reasonable.'

He laughed at her understatement. 'Yes, I like to think so.'

Miranda laughed too and their gazes locked. Instead of heat she felt light and giddy and she wanted his laughter in her life so badly it was scary.

Dear God, he really should go. She was either going to ravish him or propose to him, and both were just plain crazy.

Still, part of her wanted to prolong his visit.

'Coffee?' she asked as she stood and collected his plate. 'Or I have tea. Green or peppermint. I think I may even have some chai. Or juice.'

Good Lord, she was prattling. Just as she had that night in the lift. She willed herself to shut up but there seemed to be a weird disconnect between her brain and her tongue tonight as his gaze slowly crawled up her body and the flow of words continued at embarrassing velocity. 'I could probably even run to hot chocolate. I don't think I have marshmallows, though...'

Patrick's 'Coffee is fine' put an end to her babbling and she grabbed the chance and ran.

Thankfully, by the time she returned with two steaming mugs a couple of minutes later the verbal diarrhoea had settled. He had moved to the couch and she placed his mug in front of him. 'Black, no sugar, right?'

'Thanks,' he said.

Miranda was about to sit in her chair again when she remembered the photos she'd taken of the girls in the back yard that afternoon. 'Oh, here,' she said, slipping her phone out of her back pocket. 'I took some pics of the kids playing this afternoon.'

She scrolled to the album on her phone, sitting down next to him as she located the ones from that day. The first one she opened was of Ruby and Lola, their arms slung around each other's necks, laughing hysterically at the lens, their eyes scrunched up, their mouths open. She handed him the phone and they spent a few minutes laughing at the antics of their daughters.

The last picture was of Miranda lying on the ground with a laughing little girl lying either side of her, all three of them looking up at the camera, which she'd held at arm's length to snap the shot of them all. 'Oh, sorry,' she said, reaching for the phone. 'They wanted one with me.'

Patrick evaded her grasp as he stared at the image. It looked like any of a million snaps that made up family albums all around the country. He looked at it for a long while. This was what his daughter had missed out on—the love of a mother.

He was aware, *very* aware of the woman next to him, so close their thighs and arms were brushing.

The woman in the photo with his daughter.

'Ruby looks happy,' he said eventually.

Miranda nodded. 'She had fun.'

Patrick looked at her looking at the photo. 'You're a great mother.'

Miranda glanced up at the serious note in his

voice. His golden-brown gaze seemed troubled. 'You're a great dad.'

'I sometimes wonder if it's enough.'

She touched his arm as she had earlier and a slow burn of heat flickered to life deep and low. 'It is.'

Patrick let his gaze roam over her face, so open and honest and sexy it took his breath away. He wished he didn't want her so much.

But he did.

His gaze dropped to her mouth, remembering how good it felt to kiss her. 'You're beautiful,' he whispered. He hadn't meant to say it—they were living in an impossible situation where acting on their attraction wasn't an option.

But it came out anyway.

Miranda swallowed. The flicker became a roar. 'You're kind of beautiful yourself.'

Then his head was descending, blocking out the light, and then his lips were on hers and her head was filled with the thickness of his breath and the hammer of her pulse as she opened to him and let the roar become an inferno.

It raged out of control.

Somehow she was on her back and her hands

were pulling at his shirt, plucking at the buttons, and his were under her shirt, pushing it up, running up her ribs and pulling aside her bra, and all she could do was cling to him and cry out as his hot mouth sought first one nipple and then the other.

Then his mouth was back on hers, plundering with his tongue, and she gave up on his shirt buttons and went straight for his belt and his fly because she just had to have him inside her. She needed the pound and the thrust and the rock. It had been seven long months and she needed it. Now.

It didn't matter about the reasons why they shouldn't.

She needed it.

His tongue was laving the pulse at the base of her throat when her hand finally breached his clothing and wrapped around the hard, heavy length of him. His cry was thick and guttural and the nip of his teeth against her throat encouraged her further.

Somehow she managed to shimmy her own jeans down and wrapped her legs around his waist, bringing his blunt girth in direct contact with the heat and moisture at her centre.

'Now,' she begged, her blood thrumming through her body as her hips lifted in fevered invitation. 'Now, now, now.'

Nothing else mattered but the blinding imperative to be filled.

Patrick groaned as her heat and wetness coated him and his body demanded completion. But something fought through the pound in his head and the throb in his body. Something so ingrained in him he couldn't believe he'd come this far without giving it a thought. For God's sake, he was practically inside her without a condom in sight.

And his daughter was sleeping less than ten metres away.

Both scared the hell out of him.

'Stop,' he panted, placing his head on her chest. 'Wait.'

Miranda hadn't heard what he said over the pop and fizz in her bloodstream. All she knew was that he wasn't inside her and she mewed and clung to him, rotating her hips in blatant invitation.

Patrick pulled away before the temptation to plunge inside her became too great. 'Stop,' he said again, levering himself off her, sitting up and tucking himself back in as his brain warred with the demands of his screaming body.

Miranda blinked at the rapid halt to proceedings, not even able to move for a few moments as she tried to catch her breath and wrap her head around what had happened. Then she struggled to sit up, pulling at her jeans, yanking at her top.

'I'm sorry,' Patrick said. 'I can't do this. We... can't do this.'

Miranda knew he was right and she supposed she'd thank him for his willpower one day, for being the voice of reason, but right now her body was too busy suffering from withdrawal.

'Right,' she said. Although it didn't feel right. It felt a hundred per cent wrong.

Patrick stood and raked a hand through his hair. 'I'm sorry,' he said again.

Miranda nodded but she couldn't look at him. He may be right but for the moment that didn't really help. 'Just go, Patrick.'

'Miranda.'

She looked at him. His face was creased, his brow furrowed. She could see he was as tortured by the decision as she was. But, again, it didn't help.

'Go. Please just go.'

She didn't watch him leave, she was just grateful when the door clicked shut. Then she flopped back against the couch and curled herself into a ball.

CHAPTER FIVE

IT DIDN'T MATTER how many times he told himself he'd done the right thing, as he tossed and turned in bed, Patrick still felt like a heel. Miranda's bewilderment cut deep and the excuses rattling through his head didn't seem to matter in the dead of night, with his body craving hers like a junkie needing a fix.

Not her being twenty-two. Not his marital status. Not his utter lack of time or opportunity to indulge in a relationship. The only one that did stand up was Ruby. For the time being, he had to put her and her needs first.

The photo of Miranda laughing with Lola and Ruby came back to him, along with a rather insidious thought.

Didn't Ruby need a mother?

He quashed it immediately. Getting involved with Miranda for that reason was crazy. She deserved better. She deserved to be loved and cherished and desired for herself, not for anything she might bring to his relationship with his daughter.

And if they did get together and the wheels fell off the wagon? Was it fair on Ruby to involve her in a family, only to have that too ripped away?

Okay, she didn't remember her mother. Hell, Katie had never given their daughter a chance to get to know her. But in a world full of kids with mothers, he saw how it isolated her. Saw her longing looks and weathered her mother-related questions.

He only had to think about how attached she was already to Lola and Miranda to know he couldn't afford to gamble with his daughter's affections.

So he had to stay strong. Stay focussed.

And, if necessary, become really familiar with cold showers.

Patrick practised his apology and follow-up speech on the ten-minute drive to her place the next morning. His eyes felt gritty from lack of sleep—a seemingly permanent state for him— and he was conscious of the knot in his gut.

Before he knew it he'd arrived and he was striding up the driveway, opening the gate and heading for the covered stairs that ascended to the flat over the garage. Before he reached them, however, Miranda stepped out and both of them didn't move for a moment.

She was in cargo pants that rode low on her hips and another snug-fitting T-shirt with a V-neck that hugged the contours of her cleavage. Warm sunshine bathed her ebony hair and emphasised the shadows under her eyes. She didn't look like she'd slept well either.

Recovering first, he said, 'Good morning.'

Miranda had been determined to be cool and polite when Patrick arrived today but his damp hair, jeans and T-shirt were disturbingly casual and he looked so exhausted she forgot all about her injured pride. He'd either been awake all night. Or drinking all night.

Or both.

She planted her hands on her hips. 'How is it possible for you to look any more tired than you did last night?'

He shrugged. 'I didn't really sleep.'

Miranda's big soft heart melted at the fatigue

emanating from his every pore and lacing his voice with weariness. 'You don't look like you ever sleep.'

'I don't. Not really. Not for a very long time.'

Miranda shook her head. It was a wonder he hadn't killed anyone at work. 'Well, don't beat yourself up. You were right last night. I'm sorry, I was just...'

So freaking turned on I could barely see straight.

Patrick shook his head. 'No. Don't do that. Don't blame yourself. I'm the one who should be apologising. I shouldn't have kissed you.' He rubbed a hand along the back of his neck. 'I should have just left here as soon as I'd finished with Ruby.'

Miranda shrugged. 'A man has to eat.'

He snorted. 'I wasn't hungry for food.'

Miranda nodded. Her appetite had been pretty carnal too. There was no point being mad with him over it. They were in an untenable situation.

He took a step towards her. 'I just can't afford to be distracted from Ruby right now...she has to be my priority...'

'It's okay, Patrick,' Miranda assured him, shoving her hands in her back pockets to stop herself from her usual gesture of a comforting touch— look where that had led them in the past. 'I know exactly where you're coming from. Parents don't have the luxury of being selfish.'

Miranda knew that better than most. Getting involved with Neil a few years back had led to a painfully sticky end. Not just for her but for Lola. She wasn't keen to repeat the experience.

Even if the swirl of emotions inside her now far outweighed anything she'd ever felt for Neil.

Patrick nodded his agreement. Which was weakening by the second as Miranda's stance thrust her breasts enticingly towards him and the memory of how they tasted had his mouth watering to Pavlovian proportions, trouncing all over his resolve.

'Are the girls upstairs?' he asked, looking around, reaching for a safe topic. One on which they could both agree.

Miranda shook her head. 'They're in the house with Nan, baking cupcakes. Shall we join them?'

'Good idea,' he said, and followed her into the house.

A very good idea.

* * *

Ruby was excited to see him but she was at the delicate egg-cracking stage, tongue stuck out in concentration, so he didn't sweep her up in his arms as he usually did when he saw her after time apart.

He met Dot, who was very spritely for eighty and was fabulously patient with both the girls as she tutored them in the fine art of the perfect cupcake. She had wispy white-grey hair, a sparkle in her eyes and an easy grin.

'So you're Daddy,' she said, giving him the once-over.

Patrick smiled at her. 'I am he.'

Dot nodded thoughtfully as she looked at Miranda and back to Patrick. 'Nice,' she said, before turning her attention back to the task at hand.

'You passed,' Miranda whispered.

'I didn't know there was a test,' he whispered back.

A thoroughly enjoyable half-hour passed as they all mucked in. With two batches in the oven they all sat around the old kitchen table and iced the first two batches, which had been cooling on wire racks. Patrick feigned ignorance and Ruby very patiently explained to him the ins and outs of cake icing. Miranda and Lola seemed old hands. Dot appeared to have been born to it!

They were laughing hard, eating almost as many cakes as they'd iced.

'Watch this!' Lola called. She turned to Miranda. 'Let's show Ruby how we Eskimo-share.'

Miranda rolled her eyes. 'All right.' She picked up a cake as Lola settled on her lap then she peeled off the wrapper and held it up between their faces. Lola giggled as they both inched closer to the cake until their mouths were close enough to take a bite, which they did at the same time and munched through until they met in the middle.

Patrick laughed as Lola cracked up and crumbs went everywhere. He looked at Dot, expecting her to be disapproving of the mess, but she was probably laughing the hardest.

'Bravo! Bravo!' Dot said as Lola hugged Miranda, still laughing like she'd been hit with the giggle stick. She smiled down at Ruby. 'I think Mirry and your daddy should Eskimo-share too, don't you?'

Both girls clapped the idea enthusiastically. Miranda's eyes narrowed as she glared at her matchmaking grandmother over her daughter's head. Miranda had told Dot enough about Patrick's situation for the older woman to know that Miranda wouldn't make a scene in front of Ruby. 'Oh, I don't think so,' she said over the din.

'Oh, pleath, Daddy, pleath Ethkimo-share with Miwwy,' Ruby begged, turning impassioned eyes on her father.

'Yay, Mummy, yay!' Lola joined in.

'I think you're outvoted,' Dot said, her face the picture of innocence.

Patrick looked at Miranda. She has crumbs on her mouth and pale pink icing on her nose, and his mouth watered again.

Good God—had he contracted some drooling disorder?

He picked up a cupcake and peeled away the paper casing. 'I'm game if you are.'

She looked at her scheming grandmother. 'It's polite to share,' Dot said with an encouraging nod. 'Come here, Lols, let's stay out of their way.'

Lola didn't need to be told twice, scrambling off Miranda's lap lickety-split.

Little traitor. *Both* of them.

Miranda turned back to face Patrick, their gazes locking as he held the cake between them, his mouth slowly advancing. Hers too seemed to move of its own volition, like it knew what it wanted and wasn't afraid to go after it.

And it *wasn't* the cupcake.

Patrick didn't take his eyes off hers as his lips brushed the sponge. The excited giggles of the girls melted away, the keen gaze of a meddling old lady forgotten, the sweet perfection of the cake insignificant.

It was just a barrier to the really good stuff.

Her mouth. Her kiss.

He bit and she followed, her eyes widening, her breath the only thing he could hear despite the encouragement from their cheer squad. In seconds they were through to the middle and for the briefest moment their lips touched.

And then she pulled away.

Dropped her gaze.

Sat back.

And despite knowing it was the prudent thing to do, he felt cheated.

'Okay,' Miranda said, brushing the crumbs off

her mouth as she stood briskly and picked up dishes. 'Time to clean up.'

Dot shooed Miranda away. 'Oh, no, you sit and talk to your guest,' she said, whisking the plates away from Miranda. 'The girls and I are going to do it, aren't we?' she announced. 'That was our deal, right?'

Lola and Ruby agreed happily and Miranda and Patrick were left sitting awkwardly side by side. Patrick glanced at her. She still had icing on her nose and the drooling problem reared its ugly head again.

Screw it.

He wanted her.

It wasn't some one-off thing and he knew it. He'd always known that. He'd been trying to talk himself out of it because being with someone was another complication in a life that had been marked by them. But if he'd really come here to start again, to start afresh, why couldn't she be part of it?

'I think we should go on a date.'

Miranda glanced at him sharply. He'd kept his voice low but the determination on his face told her she hadn't misheard.

'I want you and I'm sick of denying it. But I don't want to mess about this time. I want to do it properly. Go on a date. Go on lots of dates. Like normal couples. Get to know each other. Take our time.'

Miranda cast a furtive glance towards the kitchen. Her grandmother looked away quickly. She retuned her gaze to Patrick. He looked so determined. 'No.'

'Yes.'

She shook her head. 'You were right, Patrick. You and I together is a bad idea with too much at stake.'

'That's why I want to do it right.'

Miranda shied away from the frankness in his eyes. She'd never been with a man before. She'd been with teenagers who'd looked at her with lust and eagerness. He was looking at her with the world in his eyes and all she could feel was panic.

For God's sake, he was *married!* No matter how '*technically*'.

'No.' She stood. 'Let's just leave it the way it is, okay? Please don't ask me again.'

And she scurried over to the kitchen to help clear up, whether her meddling old grandmother wanted her to or not.

An hour later Patrick and Ruby had departed with a supply of cupcakes in a plastic container and Miranda finally stopped trying to pretend she was busy.

She was standing in the back yard, supposedly watching Lola hang upside down on the monkey bars, but her thoughts were racing.

She didn't hear Dot sidle up next to her until she said, 'You should go on the date, pet.'

Miranda crossed her arms and tapped her foot. '*You* should be ashamed of yourself with your Eskimo-sharing *and* your blatant eavesdropping.'

Dot smiled, obviously *not* ashamed. 'Don't be changing the subject now.'

'What subject?' Miranda said, exasperated at her grandmother's complete lack of remorse.

'The date you're going on with Patrick.'

'I'm not going on a date with Patrick.'

'Well, you should.'

Miranda sighed. She knew her nan meant well but it really wasn't that simple. 'I can't get involved. Look what happened with Neil. Look how upset Lola was.'

'She was two,' Dot reminded her gently. 'She doesn't even remember him.'

Maybe not now but three months of happy, sunny Lola crying herself to sleep every night was not something Miranda wanted to risk again. Miranda gazed at her daughter, her icing-covered T-shirt falling down over her head. Patrick had been right earlier—they had to put their girls first.

And one of them had to be strong about that.

'He has a wife somewhere, Nan.' Even thinking about that situation rearing its head at some stage was enough to throw her off for life.

Dot touched Miranda's arm. 'Who's made it pretty clear she's out of the picture.'

'And what happens if that changes? If she comes back? I'm not going to put Lols through what I went through with Mum. I'm not going to be some other woman.'

'Hey, now, pet.' Dot put her hand on Miranda's shoulder and urged her round. 'You are not your mother.'

'Wasn't she just a victim of her circumstances?'

Dot eyeballed her. 'You're stronger than she ever was. She's my daughter and I love her, but she was always weak where men were concerned.'

Miranda laughed. She loved her grandmother's staunch loyalty. 'I slept with a guy I barely knew and got pregnant. Lot of people would say that was pretty weak.'

'No, pet. That's just human. That's just being a teenager. You were strong when it counted. You didn't lie around bemoaning your situation, getting mad, getting even, clinging to what could have been. You moved on and had Lola and you kept your schooling up and you went to university, and look at you now. I am *so* proud of my girl.'

Miranda felt suddenly teary. And old. Some days she felt bloody ancient.

'I think Patrick's a good man,' Dot pressed.

'Neil was a good man too,' Miranda countered.

'No, Neil was a boy. A nice boy, sure, but too immature to understand the demands on your attention.'

Miranda shrugged. 'He was nineteen.' They had both been. She wasn't trying to make excuses for him but it had been a lot for a nineteen-year-old to take on.

Dot nodded. 'Patrick's not.'

'We work together.'

Dot shrugged. 'So?'

'So? How am I supposed to maintain my professional integrity, keep my personal and work lives separate if I'm dating one of the anaesthetists?'

'I'm sure you'll figure out a way.'

Miranda felt at a complete loss. She was trying to be strong. Trying to do the right thing. And, as always, she needed her grandmother's support. 'Nan, please…'

Dot patted her hand. 'It's okay, pet. I know it's not been easy for you and dating Patrick wouldn't make it any more so. All I'm saying is…don't shut yourself off to the possibilities. Promise me that?'

Miranda looked into the wrinkled face so sure and gentle and wished she was small again and could curl up on her grandmother's lap. She nodded because she didn't want eighty-year-old Dot to worry. 'Okay. I promise.'

But it wasn't one she could keep.

Patrick slid the laryngoscope down along the tongue of his sedated patient and applied pressure to the handle to angle his patient's jaw open.

The light source shone down into the larynx and reflected off two white vocal cords.

Keeping his eyes firmly fixed on the cords, he held out his hand and said, 'Tube.' He hadn't even finished the word and the requested item was in his hand. He slid it down the side of the scope and pushed it through the cords, into the trachea.

'I'm in,' he said.

Fingers that he knew were painted fairy-floss pink beneath the gloves held the tube in place as he withdrew the scope and passed him a ten ml syringe. He murmured his thanks as he filled it with air and connected it to the side port, pushing in a few mls to inflate the distal cuff, anchoring it in the trachea.

Next she connected a rebreathing bag to the tube and passed it to him before efficiently tying some white tracheotomy tape around the tube and fastening it securely behind the patient's neck. He consulted the monitor, fiddled with some dials on the anaesthetic machine.

Satisfied everything was in order, Patrick pulled up his mask, which had been half on, securing the top ties before saying, 'Let's go.'

Miranda secured her mask in the same fashion

then pulled up the gurney side she'd been working from and released the brakes with a flick of her foot. She and Patrick manoeuvred it through the swing doors into operating theatre five.

Two orderlies took it from there, hefting the anaesthetised thirty-eight-year-old man about to undergo a splenectomy across to the narrow operating table. Miranda transferred the used laryngoscope and a tray of drawn-up and labelled drugs from the gurney to the stainless-steel top of the anaesthetic machine at the head of the table. Patrick removed his patient from the bag and connected him to tubing that would automatically take care of the patient's breathing for the duration of the surgery.

'Back shortly,' she said.

Miranda's hand shook as she pushed through the swing doors back into the anaesthetic room. The whole process from intubation to transfer to the table had taken less than ten minutes and even fewer words, with only the steady blip of the sats monitor to break the tension between them.

This week had been hard. Worse than the awkwardness from the beginning because then it had been as a result of what had happened between them physically. This week it had been about what had happened between them emotionally.

A much harder beast to ignore.

She knew they'd get through it, find a way to work together as time went by, but for now it wasn't so easy and avoiding him as much as possible seemed the simplest way out.

Miranda hurried to the staffroom at midday, quickly scoffing her sandwiches and cup of tea before Patrick arrived. Much to Edna's delight, she'd volunteered to spend time in the storeroom, putting away sterilised stock in the lull between morning and afternoon lists.

She'd volunteered ostensibly to familiarise herself with where every last instrument, scope, drug and suture lived but mostly to stay out of Patrick's way.

Patrick entered the staffroom as Miranda was leaving. 'Oh, hey,' he said as their bodies brushed lightly and his belly tightened. 'Ruby's nagging me about the sleepover. Should we arrange something for this weekend?'

He frowned as she barely broke stride, tossing, 'Okay sure, text me,' over her shoulder as she scurried away. He watched as her baggy scrubs moved with her rapid retreat and in ten seconds flat she'd disappeared into the storeroom.

Again.

She seemed to be spending an awful lot of time there lately.

A bunch of frustrated emotions churned in his gut and swirled in his head and he shook it to clear them as he strode into the room. Lilly greeted him as he reached the coffee machine and he chatted away for a while, sitting down with some of the nurses and joining in a conversation about some awful reality television show he hadn't subjected himself to yet.

Slowly other staff trickled in but he barely noticed. He didn't want to be here, talking to them. Any of them. He wanted to be wherever Miranda was, trying to talk some sense into her. Or at least trying to get things back on a more even footing since the date debacle.

Screw it.

He stood and excused himself, relieved to see that amidst the lively debate no one gave his departure a moment's thought as the rowdy conversation followed him out of the door. He needed to talk to her. About the sleepover, if nothing else. And if that meant cornering her in the storeroom then so be it. They couldn't go on like this indefinitely. They were colleagues. Their daughters were best friends.

He spotted her in the first compactor as soon as he entered the room. She was standing on tiptoe, struggling to shelve a large tray of instruments wrapped in the familiar blue disposable fabric that indicated their sterility.

'Allow me,' he said, advancing towards her and whisking it out of her hands before she could protest. He was aware of how close they were in the narrow space between the compactors as he reached over her head easily and placed the ENT tray on the shelf with the other ENT packs.

Miranda swallowed, her nose practically pressing into the V of his scrub top as he lifted his arms and loomed over her. She caught a whiff of the intoxicating cologne he wore and she came so close to licking him she had to take a hasty step backwards. He smelled like he had that night in the lift and that was the last thing she needed to remember, caught as she was again with him in an enclosed space.

'Thanks,' she said, her voice small.

Patrick dropped his arms. 'No worries.' He noticed how her eyes couldn't quite meet his and for the first time since they'd met, with her hair tucked under her cap and enveloped in her enormous scrubs, she actually looked her age.

Which made him feel so much better. *Not.*

'Miranda. We need to talk.'

'Yes. About the girls.' Miranda had never been so grateful for an alternative topic of conversation in her life. She shuffled her feet. Looked at a point beyond his head. 'Well, either Friday or Saturday would suit me. We'll just work in with you and Helen.'

Patrick didn't say anything, just waited and watched, refusing to look away. Refusing to pretend there weren't more important things to talk about than a play date between their girls. Sooner or later she was going to have to look at him.

Miranda's pulse tripped as the silence stretched. She stole a glance and her breath hitched at the calm, knowing look in his autumnal eyes and she couldn't look away.

Pleased he had her attention, he shook his head with deliberate slowness. 'Not about the girls.'

Miranda swallowed. There wasn't enough air or space around her as her heart raced and her brain buzzed as if she'd drunk too many glasses of wine too fast on an empty stomach. His scent and his presence morphed into a dangerous sexual cocktail.

'Us, Miranda. You and me.'

'Patrick…'

Her voice was faint, not her own, as everything shrank down to him and his lovely olive face and big broad shoulders and his wicked, sexy mouth and how very much she wanted to kiss him. And it didn't matter that they were at work, that they shouldn't, that this whole thing was crazy with a capital C.

His mouth was right there and he was staring at hers like it was a banquet and he was *starving*.

Unable to control his impulses for another moment, Patrick lifted his hand, stroked a finger down her cheek, ran a thumb over her mouth, and if she hadn't whimpered, he might just have been able to keep himself in check, but when that little desperate gurgly mew escaped, his pulse roared through his head and he was a goner.

'Damn it,' he muttered, before swooping down,

smothering the short space between them in sex and lust and primal pounding need. Sliding his hand onto her cheek, her lips opened to the demand of his. He didn't know who moaned first but he know he moaned loudest as his body demanded her total submission, flaying her mouth with a bruising kiss that pushed her against the compactor, rolling it back and back and back, taking her with it, and him following until they could go no further, and still he didn't let her up for air.

His free hand raked down her body, slid under her scrub top, sought and found a breast, and she gasped into his mouth, pushing her fullness deep into his palm.

But it was another gasp that finally, finally broke the sexual trance and they tore apart, breathing hard as they became aware they had an audience.

'Lilly,' Miranda said rather unnecessarily as she grappled to pull everything into place and pretend that they hadn't been caught making out like teenagers in the storeroom.

'Oh, I'm sorry,' Lilly said, backing away. 'Sorry...'

Miranda had one of those crazy thoughts as Lilly fled that she'd never seen the brash nurse, who lived for shock value, so gobsmacked. But it got lost in the teeming alternate reality that had taken up residence in her head.

'I don't suppose,' Patrick said as he too tried to pull his raging hormones back under control, 'there's any chance she's going to keep that to herself?'

Patrick had stopped wearing his wedding ring a few weeks back, something Lilly had quizzed him about quite closely, and she'd seemed satisfied with his vague workplace health and safety replies. But they weren't going to cut it now.

Miranda shook her head. 'None.'

He looked at her. He supposed he should be panicking but somehow he didn't care. 'Looks like we've been outed. You have to come on a date with me now. Make an honest man of me.'

Miranda didn't know whether she should laugh or cry but it felt good to know that Patrick wasn't freaking out.

In fact, neither was she.

Because Dot was right. After that kiss she

shouldn't be shutting herself off to the possibilities.

'Okay,' she said, still a little breathless, but when he smiled she smiled back and it had never felt so good to be this crazy.

CHAPTER SIX

PATRICK WAS RUNNING late. Very late. He was supposed to be picking Miranda up for their date in five minutes but he was still in his scrubs and there were a couple of patients yet to check on before he left for the night. He stripped off his theatre garb and got dressed in his suit from that morning. As he left the change rooms and headed to ICU he quickly dialled Miranda's number.

She picked up on the second ring.

'Is this where you tell me you're running late and I have to decide whether you're really running late or it's some deep psychological statement about the wisdom of what we're doing?'

Patrick smiled at the laughter in her voice. 'Nothing deep about it. The list ran over—that's it. I'm sorry but I'll be another hour by the time I do a round and go home, change and come back for you.'

'Why don't I just meet you at your place and

we can go to the restaurant from there? It'll save some time and Ruby will already be in bed.'

Patrick hesitated. It *would* save time. Miranda's place was in the opposite direction from the restaurant he'd booked. If she came to his place that would put them at the restaurant in an hour. It wasn't exactly what he'd planned for their first date. 'Are you sure? You've already picked up Lola from my place earlier today.'

'Of course,' she said. 'It makes sense.'

'Okay. Meet me there in about forty-five minutes?'

'Sure… Looking forward to it.'

Patrick was wearing a goofy grin as he pushed through the swing doors that lead to ICU.

'Did you say you were going on a date?'

Patrick steeled himself for the conversation as he undid the top two buttons of his shirt and decided to go without a tie. He looked up to where his mother-in-law stood in his bedroom doorway. 'Yes,' he said gently.

Helen didn't say anything for a moment and then managed a subdued, 'Oh.'

Patrick sighed. 'I like her, Helen. A lot.'

She nodded. 'You're married, Patrick.'

'Yes.' He shoved his hands in his pockets. 'I've been thinking it's time I did something about that.'

Helen blinked. 'A divorce?'

'Yes.'

'I see.'

'Helen...she's never coming back.' He knew Katie's mother had never stopped hoping. 'And even if she did...'

'Even if she did?' she prompted.

Patrick checked his watch. Miranda was going to be here in ten minutes—he didn't have time for this now but it had provided him the opening he'd been looking for to discuss the issue with Helen.

'Do you really think we could just pick up where we left off?' he asked, his voice soft. This had been hard on Helen too. She'd been as much a victim as he had.

'I know this has been difficult and you deserve to be happy, Patrick. You know that I think what Katie did was wrong and incredibly unfair to you and Ruby. But divorce...it's so final.'

'I know,' he acknowledged.

'I understand you wanting to move on, to be

happy, but I guess…the fact that you two were still married gave me hope that Katie might still come home. That the door was still open for her. I suppose I just can't stop hoping that she will. So another woman…it's like the end of hope, you know? It's just going to take a little adjusting to.'

'I know you've always thought deep down that she'd come back and we'd be a family again, and I've never wanted to squash that. God…if Ruby ever left without saying goodbye…'

Patrick strolled towards her as he spoke. Helen had been his rock and he owed her a lot. Any change in his life was going to affect her and he needed her to know that she didn't have to feel threatened.

'I never planned this…' God knew, he'd fought against it. 'After this mess with Katie I never thought I'd be interested in a relationship again.' He held out his arms and gathered her against his chest for a gentle hug. 'I don't know where this is going, Helen, but I want to find out.'

He felt her head nod against his chest. 'Of course. I know. I'm being silly. Just ignore me.'

He let her go. 'No, you're being a mum. A parent. We hope. That's what we do. I understand.'

Helen smiled but he swore he could see the shimmer of tears in her eyes. 'Just…be careful, okay? Don't rush in.'

'I promise.' He smiled, even though he didn't feel like it. He was sick of being careful, of being cautious. He wanted to rush in and immerse himself in the newness of it all but he'd done that with Katie and look where he was now.

A knock on the door interrupted them and Patrick grimaced. 'Can you get that? Tell her I'll be five minutes.'

He didn't wait for Helen to answer as he headed back into his bedroom. He needed to clean his teeth, put some shoes on, grab a jacket.

He felt like a teenager on his first date. His nerves tightened and butterflies danced in his stomach.

It felt good.

'Hi.' Miranda greeted Helen warmly when she opened the door. She'd been surprised earlier that day when she'd picked Lola up that Patrick's live-in help had been an older woman, but Helen had been charming and Ruby obviously adored her.

Helen gave her a stiff nod and a cool smile as

she told her to come in. 'Everything okay?' Miranda frowned.

Another nod. 'Patrick will be out shortly. Go through to the lounge.'

Miranda did as she was asked, turning to thank Helen one more time for picking up Lola from prep yesterday and putting up with her high-spirited daughter overnight, but the older woman was nowhere to be seen. Miranda's forehead crinkled at the odd reception but she let it pass as she walked around the lounge, inspecting the photos of Ruby and Patrick smiling at her from multiple frames scattered around the room.

A minute later a wolf whistle interrupted her inspection. She turned to see Patrick lounging in the archway. 'Sexy.' He smiled, looking her up and down.

Miranda grinned even as her pulse leapt at his frank perusal. She wasn't wearing anything particularly spectacular. Just a very basic red dress that she wore to most things that required some kind of effort. It was sleeveless with a modest round neckline. A slim belt at her waist cinched it in and the straightish skirt loosely followed the line of her hips and thighs. Some mascara and hoop earrings were her only adornment.

But beneath his scrutiny she felt like she was wearing a string bikini. 'You're not so bad yourself,' she returned, desperate to deflect attention from her scrunching nipples, which would be plainly evident to him if he kept staring at her like that.

'What...' he grinned looking down at his attire '...this old thing?'

Miranda laughed. He looked a hundred kinds of sexy with his shirt open to reveal the long, tanned column of his neck and the shadow of his three-day growth.

'Ready?' he asked.

She nodded as she walked towards him and when he held out his hand to her she hesitated only briefly before taking it. 'Let's go,' he murmured, and her breath hitched as his warmth enveloped her and her heart skipped a beat.

'I won't be late, Helen,' Patrick said as he passed the kitchen, where she was making herself a cup of tea.

'Okay,' she said without turning. Not that Patrick would have noticed anyway. His butterflies had taken flight and disappeared as the feel of Miranda's hand in his had instantly soothed his nerves.

Fifteen minutes later they were seated at the à la carte restaurant, looking at their menus. Light piano music tinkled discreetly in the background. Miranda ordered the risotto, Patrick the fish.

'No entrée?' he asked.

She shook her head. 'Dessert.'

'Ah, a sweet tooth?'

'What can I say? I was raised on cupcakes.'

Patrick chuckled as the waiter departed. 'Did your grandmother raise you?'

Miranda laughed. It appeared they weren't going to start with the pleasantries. 'Kind of. I spent a lot of time there growing up when my mother...'

Patrick waited for her to elaborate. She seemed to be choosing her words carefully, her gaze troubled. 'Your mother?' he prompted. 'She wasn't around?'

Miranda took a deep breath. This was the kind of thing people on dates talked about, she supposed, but it wasn't something *she* ever really talked about. 'My mother was around physically…but she had a…tempestuous relationship with my father that was…unusual and…took up a lot of mental…space.'

Patrick frowned. 'Unusual?'

Miranda sighed. If she and Patrick were going to have a relationship, he deserved more than vague references.

'She was his mistress. *The other woman*. His good-time girl. The whole boss and secretary cliché. On again, off again. With his wife. With my mother. Up then down. Moving in. Moving out. Getting divorced. Not getting divorced. Promises. Broken promises…a lot of generally unsavoury angst.'

Suddenly Miranda's virulent disgust at finding out his marital status was making a lot more sense to Patrick. No wonder she'd been mortified to discover she'd slept with a married man. 'And where did you fit into it all?'

Miranda shrugged. 'Nowhere really. He tolerated me when they were together, ignored me when they were apart. The same way he treated Mum, really. I think he resented me because I was proof of his dirty little secret.'

Patrick reached across the table and put his hand on hers. 'I'm sorry. That sounds awful.'

Miranda felt everything tingle again as his warmth and kindness reached right inside her bones. She turned her hand over and he automatically interlocked his fingers with hers. She gave him her best *qué será será* smile.

'I had Nan as a fallback. But...' Miranda thought back to her teens '...I'm afraid I rather let her down there for a while.'

Patrick squeezed her hand. 'She doesn't look let down to me.'

Miranda smiled at the truth of it. 'No.'

'So...where's your mum now? Do you have a relationship with your father?'

'He resettled in New Zealand a few years ago and my mother followed, still hoping... I don't see a lot of them really. Frankly, I can do without the continuing drama. And so can Lola.'

Patrick didn't blame her. But still he marvelled at how mature and reasonable she sounded for her age. And he realised for the first time that her age had become a non-issue. She looked gorgeous and sexy, her big silver hoop earrings brushing her neck in the exact spot he was dying to kiss, and he had an overwhelming urge to take care of her.

It was patently obvious she didn't need him or anyone else to take care of her. But he wanted to anyway.

The waiter came with their drinks and Miranda withdrew her hand, feeling suddenly self-conscious. There was a big, dangerous feeling inside her, swelling and swelling like a balloon being inflated, and when he looked at her like that, like he never wanted to let her go, it only got bigger.

And she'd never felt like this before.

She didn't know whether to run away screaming or welcome it with open arms.

He lifted his glass to her and she matched his gesture. 'To us,' he said.

Miranda felt the balloon fill a little more. 'To us.'

Why did things have to be so complicated?

It was time to lay her cards on the table. If there was ever going to be an 'us' she needed to go into it with some ground rules. It might be a little heavy for a first date but there wouldn't be any point having a second if they couldn't talk about the unique issues facing them.

She'd seen her mother's hopes continually crushed because she'd been too scared to ask for what she needed, and she wouldn't let it happen to her. Or Lola.

'Uh-oh,' Patrick joked as he watched her face grow serious. 'Something tells me you're thinking too much.'

Miranda took a deep breath. 'Can I ask you why you've never got a divorce?'

It was something she'd pondered for a while now but hadn't considered it her business. But if he was going to make good on those promises in his eyes, then for damn sure it was about to be her business.

Best to get it out now.

Thanks to years of listening to her mother's rants she knew more about divorce law than a lot of lawyers. You didn't need both parties to agree to a divorce these days. All you needed was a separation. And Patrick had that in spades.

Patrick placed his drink carefully on the table as the hard-hitting question socked him right between the eyes. He couldn't believe she'd brought this topic up not long after he'd had the same conversation with Helen.

'I…don't know, to be honest.' He played with the frost beading the outside of his glass. 'For a while part of me hoped, wondered, dreamed that Katie would come back and we'd be a family again. That Ruby would have her mother back.'

He looked up at her. 'Then time passed and I was busy with Ruby and work and life and it became a matter of timing. Of doing it when she came back because it seemed cowardly to do it in absentia. And then some more time went by and my marital status has been a kind of a security blanket, if anything, and suddenly it's five years later…'

Miranda nodded. God knew, she understood how time passed in a blur when your child was young. But, still, she had to start as she meant to go on. 'I'm not going to get involved with a married man.'

Patrick nodded. Given what she'd just told him, he understood perfectly. There was a candle in the middle of the table and there was a flickering glow all over her face, her eyelashes forming shadows on her cheeks. 'It's just…not easy with Helen. Funnily enough, I mentioned the D word to her just before you arrived and…well…

let's just say it's probably going to take her a little while to get used to—'

'Helen?' Miranda frowned as she interrupted. 'Your nanny has some kind of investment in whether you divorce or not?'

Patrick blinked. *She didn't know?* 'Helen is my mother-in-law.'

His mother-in-law? *Katie's mother?* Miranda wondered for a moment if she'd misheard but he was looking at her so openly she knew she hadn't. A sudden swell of anger rose in her chest. 'You don't think you could have told me that?'

Patrick frowned. 'I thought you knew.'

Miranda racked her brains, trying to find the time he'd told her that vital piece of information but couldn't. She'd heard Ruby talk about her grandmother quite a bit but she just hadn't made the connection. And this afternoon she'd merely introduced herself as Helen.

'No. But it certainly explains Helen's rather cool greeting this evening. Especially when I rocked up just after you mentioned divorcing her daughter.'

'Helen was cool with you?'

'Oh, yeah.' She nodded.

'That doesn't sound like her.'

An old itch, one she hadn't felt in a long time, crawled up her spine. Her father had done that when he'd been defending his wife against some accusation made by her mother.

He'd sucked at trying to keep two women in check.

Miranda raised her glass to her mouth and made sure he was looking right at her before she said, 'She was cool.'

He nodded as he watched her glossy lips close around her straw. 'I'll talk to her about it.'

Miranda almost choked on her drink. 'What?' she gasped as she replaced the drink with a clatter on the table. The last thing she wanted was to make trouble.

'You're important to me, Miranda. I don't want her treating you like a pariah because of a whole bunch of stuff that happened five years ago that wasn't your fault and over which you had no control.'

Miranda was touched by his defence of her but a part of her sympathised with Helen, just as part of her had always sympathised with her father's wife. *She* was moving in on claimed territory—it was up to *her* to tread carefully.

'Patrick, *of course* she's going to feel some animosity towards me. She's probably spent the last five years harbouring reunion fantasies in her head and now here I am, threatening that and her place in your family. Do *not* say a word to her.'

She reached out her hand this time and touched his.

'Let's just give her some time, okay? I'm sure she doesn't want you to be alone for the rest of your life.'

Patrick smiled and then shook his head and broke into a chuckle.

'What?' she asked, eyeing him dubiously but smiling anyway because his low, sexy laughter was contagious.

'You,' he said. 'You are wise beyond your years, do you know that?'

'Oh, don't,' she groaned. 'Don't make me feel any more ancient than I do. I'm rather afraid I'm not some fun, peppy, energetic twenty-two-year-old who's up for anything. Especially on a school night.'

Miranda didn't often feel like she'd missed out

on those crazy teen years—mostly she was just too tired to think about it. But occasionally she did wonder how her life would have turned out if she hadn't been pregnant at seventeen.

Patrick laughed at her joke but sobered quickly. 'I've had young and peppy. Trust me, it's not all it's cracked up to be.'

They gazed at each other for a long moment, both reflecting on what they'd experienced in the past and knowing somehow that they were embarking on something so much better.

'The risotto for the lady?' the oblivious waiter asked, interrupting their moment.

Patrick nodded, dragging his gaze away. 'Yes, thank you.'

They ate their meal sticking to safer topics about the food and the restaurant. As they finished and the waiter took their plates the conversation moved to the gossip at work that had already begun to circulate about them, especially now Patrick had confessed to Lilly that not only was he separated but he was *the* Dr Costello who'd been briefly accused of murdering his wife five years ago.

Patrick shook his head. 'Hospitals are the same

wherever you go. All about the gossip. I'm sorry you're going to get caught up in the fallout.'

Miranda laughed. 'My mother was a *mistress*. Trust me, I'm pretty familiar with gossip.' She thought back to some of the things the kids at school had said, which had only added to the general unhappiness of her childhood. 'I bounced back from that, I'm sure I'll weather this too. Don't worry about me. I bounce. I'm a survivor.'

Patrick arched an eyebrow. 'And if things don't work out between us? Will you bounce back from that too?' It didn't bear thinking about but it was a possibility. Something they had to talk about before they went down the track he was being tugged down by a power he didn't understand.

Miranda doubted it. There was a whole well of emotions inside her already associated with him. She hadn't wanted to get too close, examine them in any detail for the exact reason he'd just given. 'I don't know,' she said honestly. 'Neil I could survive but you…'

Patrick quirked an eyebrow. 'Wait… Neil?'

Miranda faltered. The name had slipped out without thought. 'Neil was a guy I lived with for about six months when Lola was two.'

Patrick sat back in his chair, surprised. 'Oh. I didn't realise there'd been anyone else.'

Miranda nodded. 'We were nineteen. He was a fellow student nurse. He was funny and Lola adored him and I think I wanted to give her a normal family life so desperately I didn't see any issues with involving him in our lives. And he was great with Lols and he fitted right in. But...'

Miranda looked at him watching her, his olive complexion accentuated by the low light. 'He was nineteen. The glow of family life eventually dimmed. He tried hard, I know that and I don't blame him for wanting to have some fun and live a little, but I couldn't. I had responsibilities. I couldn't go out to clubs all night. Or drop everything for some party.'

'So he left?'

Miranda nodded. 'Eventually. And I understood that.'

'You weren't angry or upset?'

Miranda gazed into the candle. 'I was upset about it, of course, but...not devastated. Lola, on the other hand...'

Miranda shuddered just thinking about how distraught her daughter had been when Neil had walked out. She raised her eyes to his. 'I was naïve. I thought it would be fine to bring someone into her life like that. I can't be that naïve again, Patrick. I can't enter into a relationship and have it just be about me. I need to be cautious. I need to be sure. And so do you.'

Patrick nodded. He knew exactly what she meant. The stakes were high and they were both aware of the consequences. But he'd never been surer. 'I am.'

'Then you need to get a divorce.'

She hated the way her quiet statement was haunted with the echoes from her childhood. How she sounded like her mother demanding over and over that her father divorce his wife. But she wasn't demanding, she was asking. And she was only going to ask once.

He nodded. 'I know.'

Their gazes locked and the sincerity in his eyes was breathtaking. Miranda felt it down to her bones.

The oblivious waiter returned, breaking the spell. 'Dessert?'

They drove home in silence half an hour later and in the confines of the car Miranda had never been more aware of him. Her peripheral vision was full of him. His strong thigh, the rise and fall of his chest, his spicy scent with that lingering sweetness intoxicating her senses until she was almost dizzy with wanting to bury her face in his neck and inhale.

Her breath was thick in her lungs and it stuttered into the laden air like heavy fog.

Patrick glanced at her. 'Stop,' he said.

She swallowed at the hunger she saw in his gaze. 'Stop what?'

He looked back at the road, his hand gripping the gear stick hard because if he let go it would be on her knee. Then it would be under her skirt. And then, God help him, he'd be screeching the car to the side of the road. 'Stop thinking what you're thinking.'

Miranda didn't ask how he knew what she was thinking because she had a feeling they were on the same wavelength. She just dragged her eyes off him, her heart pounding, and resolutely turned to look out her window.

He pulled up in his double driveway next to her car ten minutes later. Neither of them moved. But within seconds steamy thoughts had led to hot breaths that started to fog the inside of the car.

Patrick turned to face her. 'I meant what I said. I want to do this differently this time around. The first time…ending up in bed so soon… If we're going to get this right, we need to take it slower.' His gaze drifted to the pulse fluttering at the base of her throat. 'I think we should date a little first, really get to know each other before we take it to an…' her chest rose and fell, stretching the fabric of her dress in interesting ways '…intimate level.'

Although that horse had already bolted, Miranda understood his reasoning. She nodded, wishing he wouldn't look at her like he wanted to tear her dress off and that the word 'intimate' hadn't put a whole bunch of pictures in her head.

'Good idea,' she said, and cleared her throat of the ridiculous wobble it seemed to be suddenly plagued with.

Patrick felt his loins heat at the low, throaty lilt to her voice. His eyes roved over her face. There was colour in her cheeks. And her mouth… He looked away from her mouth, concentrated on the steering-wheel.

'And we should definitely keep it from the girls. We need to be sure ourselves first.'

Miranda nodded vigorously. 'Agreed.' *Definitely.* They absolutely needed to be sure before the girls became involved.

Her gaze fanned over his neck, where his open collar brushed a pulse bounding to a steady beat. The urge to press her lips there, to taste the heat and the sweetness of him, rocked through her and she dropped her gaze.

To his thigh. His solid, virile thigh. That had pressed her to a mattress and draped over her, imprisoning her in his arms.

She dragged her gaze up and their eyes met. She swallowed as her pulse beat a desperate tempo through her blood. 'So what's next?' she asked in that annoying alto again.

Patrick drew in a ragged breath at the desire smoking her gaze to a sizzle. 'Clandestine dating.' He looked at her mouth again. So soft, so tempting. 'No sex.'

Miranda rode a surge of thwarted desire. He smelled so good and she just wanted a tiny, tiny taste of him. Something to get her through. What if they never got to the intimacy level? What if after a few dates it was just too hard and they decided to drop it?

She shut her eyes briefly to dispel the terrible thought. 'Right. Agreed,' she said. 'We date. No sex. Technically you're still married and we need to take it slowly. Be sure. For us *and* the girls.'

'Agreed,' he said, dragging his gaze from her mouth. 'Dating only. No…sex.'

Miranda swallowed at the way he said 'sex'. One part grim determination, nine parts yearning. She twisted in her seat a little. 'Do you think we should clarify the…physical boundaries?'

Patrick frowned as he too turned a little to face her. 'Miranda.'

Miranda liked the way he said her name like that. With a tiny note of warning. Arousal flushed through her like an injection of vodka directly into her veins. 'No. I mean, no sex is fairly broad…right?'

Patrick nodded, starting to feel really, really hot as Miranda seemed to loom a little closer. 'It means no kissing,' he murmured, as he thought about doing just that and her mouth drew his gaze. 'No fondling.' He could hear the loudness of his breath as he thought about that too. 'Absolutely no fondling...'

Miranda nodded, her gaze drawn to his mouth. 'What about just touching, though?' she asked, and her hand trembled as she slid it onto his thigh.

Patrick's flesh leapt at her touch, his pulse hammered at his temples. 'Stop, Miranda,' he warned, his gaze still on her mouth, which seemed closer now. Had she moved or had he?

Miranda couldn't stop. All she could think about was his taste, all she could hear was the demanding whisper in her head to relive it. She inched her mouth closer, her hand higher on his thigh. It was dark and cosy in the fogged-up car—like their own little bubble.

'Too intimate?' she whispered, her gaze zeroing in on his lips, her mouth watering as she felt his breath on hers.

'Miranda,' he groaned, slipping his hand onto her cheek, pushing his fingers into her hair.

His mouth whispered against hers just as the car filled with blinding white light and they leapt apart at the startling intrusion.

Patrick ran a hand through his hair, his chest pounding with a mix of desire and adrenaline.

'I think Helen is sending a message,' he said, breathing hard.

Miranda blinked, appalled at her lack of control as she too tried to pull herself back from the edge and master her frantic pulse and heavy breathing. 'I'd better go...' She fumbled for the door handle with one hand, grabbing for her bag with the other.

Patrick didn't stop her. The fact they could so easily have been making out in his car right now like randy teenagers shook him to the core. For crying out loud—he was parked in a car outside his house while his five-year-old daughter was asleep inside!

Hardly father of the year material.

Moments later Miranda backed out of his driveway and took off like a bat out of hell. Patrick placed his head on the steering-wheel and banged his forehead against it several times for good measure.

CHAPTER SEVEN

AND THEY WERE good. So good. For four weeks. Four long weeks where, thanks to Helen and Dot, they went on clandestine dates and behaved impeccably. Patrick chose crowded places and they took two cars. They didn't so much as hold hands. They just enjoyed each other's company. Laughed and talked and relaxed.

As much as two people who wanted to rip each other's clothes off could relax.

They also kept it strictly professional at work despite the gossip swirling around them and Lilly's best efforts to ascertain the status of their relationship. Even in front of the girls they kept up a polite and friendly veneer.

Lola and Ruby were becoming inseparable and as heartening as it was to see their girls getting on so well together, it also served as a reminder to Patrick and Miranda to keep their priorities straight. If they stuffed the relationship up, they wouldn't be the only casualties. Two little girls would also suffer.

On their one-month anniversary Patrick picked Miranda up in a limo after decreeing earlier that day she wear a pretty dress and her dancing shoes. Miranda gaped at the sleek white machine that beckoned from the kerb.

'Are you sure?' she said, already swooning over the tux that clung to his broad shoulders and thinking about what they could accomplish in the back of such a decadent ride. 'It looks like it might be hard to stick to the whole no-sex thing inside that.'

Patrick looked at her with a faux horrified expression. 'I can assure you, as your prom date, my intentions are completely honourable.'

Miranda couldn't quite believe what she'd heard. 'Prom date?' she said, trying to keep the tremor of excitement out of her voice.

He grinned. 'Dot told me you never got to yours.'

She shook her head as a surge of something big and hot welled in her chest. 'No, I didn't.'

He opened the door for her. 'Then your carriage awaits.'

Once inside Patrick produced a corsage of tiny white roses and placed it on her wrist. Miranda stroked the delicate petals. 'It's beautiful,' she said, looking into his eyes.

Patrick shook his head. 'You're beautiful.'

They stared at each other for long moments until a voice from the front said, 'Are you sure you don't want me to put the partition up, sir?'

Patrick dragged his gaze from Miranda's delectable face. 'Positive, thanks, Larry. We're going to need a chaperon.'

The chauffeur laughed and said, 'Right you are, sir.'

The limo pulled away from the kerb and Miranda said, 'Where are we going?'

Patrick just smiled. 'Patience, prom queen, patience.'

Three quarters of an hour later they rolled to a stop in a hilly wooded area. Larry waited with the parked limo while Patrick led Miranda through some trees to a small clearing already set out with a picnic blanket and lit on the perimeter by hanging paper lanterns. A gentle breeze caressed her skin and the city lights twinkled in the distance.

Miranda gasped. 'Patrick, this is amazing.'

He smiled as he leaned down and pushed a button on the portable CD player that sat beside the champagne bucket. A nineties rock ballad rose around them. 'Shall we dance?'

Miranda took his hand, her heart overflowing. 'I feel like I'm seventeen again,' she said.

Patrick pulled her close. 'Good.'

Three hours later they'd eaten a feast of gourmet finger food, boogied until their feet hurt, laughed and talked and were on their way back to reality.

'Thank you, Patrick,' Miranda said as he saw her to her door and they were standing like teenagers before it. The temptation to yank him inside and check out what she knew to be pretty magnificent man-flesh beneath his tuxedo was overwhelming. 'That was so much fun.'

Patrick's breath caught at the sheen of excitement he could still see in her eyes and felt an answering thrill inside him to know that he'd been the man to put it there. To give her an experience she'd never had before. It *had* been fun. He never really got the chance to let his hair down any more. But he had tonight.

'My pleasure,' he murmured resolutely.

Miranda smiled at him as her pleasure detector soared off the charts. She took a step closer to him, her breath rough in her lungs. 'I know we're keeping our hands off each other but I do believe that a prom date is not complete without a goodnight kiss?'

Patrick swallowed. He knew that look. God knew, he wanted to push her against the door and give her more than a kiss. But he was determined to give her the entire prom experience so instead he delivered a chaste kiss to her cheek and ignored her tiny mew as he pulled back slowly.

'Goodnight,' he whispered, then turned away, heading down the stairs to home and yet another cold shower.

Two days later a lift Miranda had been waiting for opened. It was groaning with people who stood looking at her and waiting for her to get in, and the only spot available was next to one Patrick Costello. He winked at her as he leant nonchalantly back against the wall.

'Room for you here,' he said, as he shuffled over as far as the cramped conditions allowed.

Miranda felt sure every occupant of the lift must have been able to hear the rapid rat-a-tat of her heart as she squeezed in beside him. She felt the instant sweep of his little finger against hers, as deceptively innocent as their prom-night kiss and a slow burn flared in her belly.

She concentrated nervously on the other occupants of the lift. There was a man in pyjamas sporting an IV pole and a packet of cigarettes. An orderly in charge of a wheelchair carrying an elderly woman and beside him a nurse with a chart tucked against her side. Miranda smiled absently at the nurse.

There were two women she assumed to be sisters talking in muted undertones about a nursing-home placement for their father. Several other people appeared to be at St Bennie's by themselves, staring silently at the numbered display as the lift counted down the floors.

Slowly the lift emptied. The orderly and the nurse accompanying the wheelchair got out at X-Ray, along with two others. The smoker and another two got out at level five, which led out to an area of garden where people still smoked despite hospital policy.

By the time the lift doors slid shut with two floors to go until the OR level, they were finally alone. They didn't separate. Patrick smiled down at her. 'And then there were two.'

He reached across the front of her and punched the emergency button. The lift jerked to a halt, the bell clanging urgently.

Miranda swallowed at his predatory look, the noise fading from her mind. He had hat hair and a still visible red mark across the bridge of his nose from his mask. But she wanted him.

'What are you doing?'

Patrick swung round, trapping her body against him and the lift wall. One hand cupped her cheek, the other slid onto her hip and pulled her close. 'I can't stand it a second longer. I haven't been able to think about anything else since the prom.'

He exhaled on a rush of lust, his head swooping, his mouth opening over hers, his tongue stroking along her bottom lip, his pulse roaring through his ears.

He groaned as she let him in on a whimpery inhalation, her hand reaching for his tie and yanking him closer, urging him to go deeper. He obliged, and her perfume filled his senses, her head bumping against the wall as he allowed his lust full reign.

The bell rang and rang and rang and they were oblivious.

It was a different ring, the urgent burst of the emergency telephone, that finally cut through their raging passion.

Patrick stepped back, hands on hips, his chest heaving as he stared at her, her mouth swollen and wet from his kisses. Her smoky gaze was dazed, her breasts stretching her T-shirt as she gasped to grapple back control of her breathing.

'I think we need to revise the no-touching policy,' he said, clearing his throat and ignoring the phone.

Miranda nodded dumbly, her brain still short-circuiting. After that kiss she wondered if they should just scrap it altogether. 'Yes.'

Patrick nodded. 'Good.'

Their gazes locked as he reached for the phone. He snatched it up without taking his eyes off her and Miranda watched him watching her as he talked to the person on the other end.

'Sorry,' he apologised, although his eyes told her he wasn't sorry at all. 'We're fine...' He smiled at her and her stomach flopped. 'Something came up. I'm releasing the emergency stop button now.'

Still holding her gaze, he hung up the phone and hit the red button. The lift lurched obediently into action and he used the movement to bring them closer again, swooping in again for a quick, hard, kiss to her mouth, pulling away slightly as the lift dinged.

'Until tomorrow night,' he murmured against her mouth, then turned away from her in time to be standing neutrally, as if they hadn't just been necking in a lift, when the doors opened.

Miranda let out a husky breath as the doors closed, completely missing her stop.

Tomorrow night. Their date tomorrow night. Her belly went into free-fall.

As it turned out, she didn't have to wait that long.

Her phone rang at eleven that night, calling her back to work for a craniotomy coming from ICU.

As part of her roster, Miranda worked three days out of the month on call, which involved three one p.m. to nine p.m. shifts in a row and going on call immediately after each one ended until six a.m. the following morning.

Luckily for Miranda, she had her grandmother to fall back on. It made things easier in the middle of the night to know that Lola was tucked up safely in Nan's house.

Half an hour later she was back in her scrubs, setting up for the incoming extradural haematoma. The swing doors opened and Patrick sauntered in, looking sexier in pink than any man had a right to.

'Morning,' he murmured, sidling up beside her in the anaesthetic room, his butt resting against the hip-high bench. 'So this is what you look like in the wee hours.'

He smiled down at her and Miranda smiled back as his eyes crinkled nicely. 'You know damn well what I look like in the *wee hours,* Patrick Costello.'

'Oh, that's right.' He grinned. 'So I do. It's been so long you might have to jog my memory.'

Miranda quirked an eyebrow. 'We're *drastically* revising the policy, then?'

Patrick watched Miranda's mouth as it formed the words. It had tasted so good earlier today he'd been craving it ever since. 'I thought maybe we could…move on to kissing?'

Miranda's mouth felt on fire as his gaze zeroed in, stroking heat along it. She was aware of their arms brushing, the closeness of his hip, his thigh. 'And you think we'll be able to stop at just kissing?'

'Hmm,' he mused as his craving kicked up another notch. 'Good point.'

The phone on the wall rang and Miranda laughed. It seemed they were forever going to be interrupted by phones. She reached over and picked it up. It was ICU.

'They're ready for us,' she told him as she replaced the receiver thirty seconds later and pulled her traitorous body back into line. For now she had a job to do and it didn't involve crushing on Patrick.

They had a life to save. Nothing else mattered at the moment.

The operating theatres connected to the ICU via a swing door and Miranda and Patrick, along with another nurse and two orderlies, entered the unit a minute later and walked down the corridor that led to the main area.

A nurse bustled past them on her way to the storeroom. 'Bed eight,' she said, without breaking stride.

It was the first time Miranda had been to ICU and she wasn't prepared for it. The unit was lit up like a Christmas tree and was a hive of activity. A swarm of people already surrounded the bed and they joined them.

The ICU team launched into their handover. 'This is seventeen-year-old Candice Halifax, who got into a fight tonight at a party and fell, hitting her head on the gutter.'

Miranda took nothing in after that. She glanced at the young woman pale and unmoving in the bed surrounded by a host of medical technology. An older woman, a relative perhaps, stood still beside the bed in the midst of all the activity, her back bent and bowed, tears streaming down her face, clutching the patient's hand.

She chose that moment to look up and caught Miranda's gaze. 'She's not a bad kid,' she said to Miranda, her gaze beseeching. 'She's been going through a rough trot at home, that's all.'

Miranda looked back at Candice and felt as if she'd been punched. The girl had an endotracheal tube in her mouth, which was connected to a ventilator, and a slight red mark on her temple. She had blonde hair and a sprinkling of freckles across her nose. She looked young and pretty. She looked…asleep.

She'd been Candice.

Confused, unhappy, rebellious. She'd consumed alcohol. She'd gone to wild parties. Been reckless. Acted like she was bulletproof.

And she'd always thought she'd paid heavily for her rebellion. After all, she'd fallen pregnant.

She could still hear her mother's scathing condemnation when she'd finally confessed the pregnancy. Looking at Candice lying still and near death, words that she'd thought were in her past blasted into her brain with all the ferocity of dynamite.

Stupid, stupid little slut! I knew this was going to happen with your drinking and your partying and your skipping school. I knew some guy was going to knock you up. Your father said you were out of control. How's this going to look to him now? Get out. Get out and don't ever come back.

So she'd left and gone to live with her grand-mother and had had Lola and her life had been turned upside down. But looking at Candice now, she knew she'd got off easy. That there were even harsher realities. She hadn't paid for her teenage stupidity with her life. She hadn't ended up in Intensive Care with someone about to cut into her head. She hadn't been on some critical list with a dangerous blood clot threatening her existence.

But she could have been.

Nausea threatened as the knowledge hit home. They had to save Candice. They just had to.

'Miranda?'

Miranda was dragged back to the present by Patrick's voice. Obviously handover was finished as the orderlies started to manoeuvre the bed out of its area and get Candice to Theatre.

He frowned down at her. 'You okay?'

She nodded, moving automatically with the bed. 'Let's just save her, okay?'

He gave her a grim nod. 'I'm not losing any-one tonight.'

But they nearly did. There was extensive bleed-ing from Candice's head when they opened her up, much more than anyone was expecting, and finding the arterial bleeder was difficult when the operative field was obscured by all the blood. It soaked into the sterile drapes and dripped onto the floor.

The atmosphere was tense as the team worked to pull Candice across the line and two hours later Miranda was exhausted from running back and forth for blood products, drawing up infusions, administering fluids. Not to mention the mental energy and concentration she'd expended, willing Candice to be okay.

You can do it, Candice. You can do it. Stay with us. Just stay with us.

When they pushed her back into her bed space in ICU no one was sure if Candice would make it through the night.

But Miranda had to believe she would and as she helped clean up the theatre she refused to believe that she wouldn't. Candice had her whole life ahead of her—surely it wasn't going to be snatched away?

She met Patrick at the change-room doors, the male and female rooms being side by side. He'd stayed in ICU for a while.

'How is she?'

'Her intracranial pressure's pretty high still,' he said.

He was different from the man who had flirted with her just a few hours ago. His eyes were a little bloodshot and the lines around his mouth were more noticeable. He'd fought hard to keep Candice alive as she'd bled and bled and he looked totally exhausted.

'Will she make it?'

Patrick shrugged. 'She lost a lot of blood...'

Miranda nodded, knowing that no one could predict Candice's outcome at the moment, but it still didn't stop her wanting to hear that everything was going to be okay. 'Do you want to come to mine?'

Adrenaline had surged through her system as they'd fought the good fight for Candice but now they'd done their part and it was all over Miranda was left feeling jittery and wrung out. Not to mention the memories and emotions it had stirred up from her own teenage years. And her mother's terrible words.

She didn't want to be alone with them.

Hell, she just wanted to wrap herself in his arms and go away to some place where none of the world existed. Not teenage troubles. Not single motherhood. Not work or home or the girls.

Just him and her.

Patrick's pulse leapt. It was pretty clear from her frank gaze that she wasn't talking about a cup of hot chocolate between colleagues. But still he hesitated. She wasn't some bar pick-up tonight. 'Are you sure?'

Miranda nodded. 'Yes. I don't want to be alone tonight.'

'Not that many hours left before sunrise,' he murmured.

She shrugged. 'I'll take them.'

Patrick's loins stirred. 'What about Lols?'

'She's at Nan's.'

He lifted his hand to cup her face and his gut squeezed as she rubbed her cheek against his palm. 'Give me half an hour. I'm going to get dressed and go back and check on Candice.'

Miranda smiled as she fell just a little bit in love, despite telling herself she wouldn't. 'Come when you can. I'll be waiting.'

It was almost three-thirty when Miranda heard Patrick's footsteps on her stairs. She'd been lying on the couch in a semi-drowse. Her pulse picked up as he knocked and she swung her feet over the side. Her legs felt weak as she made her way to the door. The satin of her floor-length gown had been cool when she'd slipped it on her freshly showered naked skin almost an hour ago but it was warm and moved against her now like a lover's caress.

She had contemplated putting underwear on but hadn't wanted the hindrance or the extra time it would take to get out of it. Patrick wasn't coming over at three in the morning to exchange pleasantries.

He'd better not be anyway!

She opened the door and he was leaning against the jamb in track pants and a T-shirt and he smiled at her, his gaze drifting to the way the gown sat wide on her shoulders and low on her cleavage. 'I think I'm overdressed,' he murmured.

She smiled back, suddenly feeling stupidly nervous. Maybe she should have worn more. 'Hi.'

'Hi, back.'

She stepped aside to let him pass. 'How's Candice?'

Patrick sauntered in, lights from the street outside poking fingers of light into the darkened room. He turned to face her, shoving his hands in his pockets. Her gown looked silky soft and he knew where they'd rather be. 'Still unstable. They're giving her some mannitol.'

Miranda shut the door, sagging against it at the progress report. She'd hoped he'd arrive with better news.

Patrick took a couple of steps towards her. The room may have been dark but her troubled smoky-green gaze seemed luminous. 'She got to you, didn't she?'

Miranda nodded. Patients always had but Candice had been a little too close for comfort. 'That could have been me,' she said.

He lifted his hand, smoothed her fringe back with his fingers and trailed them down her cheek. 'But it wasn't.'

'I was like her. Young. Off the rails. Desperate for someone to pay me attention.'

Patrick stroked his thumb along her bottom lip, watched as her nipples beaded against the fabric of her gown. Her brow was furrowed, her gaze concerned. He leaned in and kissed her forehead. 'Shh,' he whispered.

Miranda felt tears prick at her eyes at his gentleness and she shut them. The soft press of his lips calmed and stirred her in equal measure. 'I was so lucky.'

At the time she hadn't thought getting pregnant with Lola had been lucky but she had no idea where she'd be now if the responsibility hadn't been foisted on her.

He kissed each closed eyelid. 'Shh,' he whispered again.

A tear squeezed out from under an eyelid and he kissed it away. Kissed her on the nose, the side of the mouth, along her jaw and down one side of her neck. His tongue lapped at the pulse that bounded in her throat and she gasped as her skin practically sizzled and heat unfurled through her veins.

Candice faded. Her own dice with danger faded. The tears faded. And the thud took over. The thud and the pound and the roar as her pulse beat hard and insistent, washing lust and desire through her veins, stroking it over her breasts, fanning it through her belly, whispering it between her legs.

His mouth found its way to hers and she opened

to him on a moan and when moments later he pushed a thigh between her legs, pinning her against the door, she welcomed that with a moan too, settling on his thigh, feeling him thick and hard against the place that ached and tingled.

Her gown gaped open and she didn't care. She wanted it open, she wanted it off. She wanted him to strip it away and put the tongue that was currently playing peek-a-boo with hers all over her body.

Patrick broke away, his hand still cupping her jaw as his pulse screamed out a demand for more. But Miranda seemed fragile tonight and he wanted it to be slow and lazy. Wanted to treat her with the gentleness that had been missing from her life for a long time, usurped, as it had been, by the yoke of responsibility.

'Better?' he murmured, his thumb sweeping along her cheek.

Miranda prised lust-drunk eyes open. 'Yes.'

He smiled. 'Good.'

Patrick dropped his gaze to her gown. It had fallen off one shoulder and parted and opened where his leg was shoved high and hard between hers. He reached for the belt and pulled at the loose knot. The gown fell completely open and his gaze feasted on her breasts. 'Nice,' he whispered.

Miranda blushed at his intense stare, her nipples showing no shame at all as they ruched right in front of him.

He trailed his hand down from her jaw, running over her collar bone and lower until it was brushing over a nipple, which grew even harder. His other hand moved to claim the neglected side.

'I like the way they do that,' he mused, his eyes fixed on the enticing swing of her lovely full breasts.

Miranda felt his lazy touch arrow all the way to the spot where his thigh met her centre and she gasped as he lowered his head and sucked one nipple deep into his mouth. She shut her eyes as she fought the urge to grind herself against him with every sweep of his hot tongue.

'So...' she panted, 'we've moved past the kissing stage too?'

Patrick raised his head, claiming her mouth in a bruising kiss that left her boneless as his hands worked their magic on her breasts.

'Nope,' he said against her mouth. 'I'm going

to kiss you a lot.' He pressed his mouth on hers again, using his tongue to taste her as he went. 'Everywhere,' he muttered, going in for another. 'Until the sun comes up.'

When he kissed her this time she joined him, her hands sliding around his neck, pulling him down hard, stroking her tongue against his, rubbing herself along his thigh as the thrum in her blood built to fever pitch.

She grasped his shirt and pulled it up over his head, her palms tingling with pure sensual delight as they revelled in the smoothness of his broad shoulders. She moaned as her aching nipples grazed erotically against the hair on his chest with each rock of her pelvis against his thigh. Her body was following a rhythm it couldn't deny and his was stoking it as he bit gently on her neck.

Suddenly the hard jut of probing fingers joined the heat and the wet between her legs and she opened her eyes on a gasp, her head falling back. 'If you do that I'll…'

Patrick looked her straight in the eyes. 'Come,' he whispered. 'Come.' And claimed her mouth one more time.

Miranda whimpered, unable to stop the rhythmic rock of her hips or the way she pushed hard against his hand hitting the right spot over and over and over.

And quickly, too quickly, wrapped up in the havoc of his mouth and his tongue and the headiness of his breath loud in her head, the edges of her world started to unravel and an orgasm slammed into her with all the might and fury of a hurricane.

She cried out, her head falling back as everything tightened then splintered around her, pleasure so close to pain drenching every cell in a frantic jungle call as she came and she came and she came.

Patrick kissed her as she floated down from the high, bussing her face and her neck with fluttery offerings, and then, without giving her a chance for her world to fully right itself, he swung her up in his arms.

Her arms linked around his neck and he liked it as she asked, 'Where are we going?' in a voice that sounded more than a little high.

'Bedroom,' he said. 'I haven't finished with you yet.'

He kissed her all the way there, navigating blindly, banging into every piece of furniture she owned but eventually making it and throwing her on the bed, watching her look at him with lust and wonder.

And then he was joining her, settling between her legs and licking her there, and she gasped, raising her head off the bed.

'Patrick. No...you don't have to... I...'

But her feeble protest died as lust flared to life again and her head fell back as he continued to stroke her with his tongue, and soon she was lost and building again, an urgent hand in his hair as she stiffened and cried out, and he didn't stop until she was spent and begging him for mercy.

So he stopped. But just long enough to divest himself of his jeans and underwear, his throbbing erection springing free as he pulled a condom out of his pocket.

Miranda watched him, half her brain in some place that existed up in the stars, the other half already anticipating how good he was going to feel. She opened her arms to him, urging him to hurry, and when he finally settled on top of her it was the most natural thing in the world to wrap her legs around his waist, to raise her hips and say, 'Now.'

He groaned into her neck as he entered her and he felt so good filling her, she held him tightly in place, refusing to let him thrust for a moment, just wanting to be filled and stretched, their hearts beating as one.

But soon the demands of her own body, the nerves that were still hyper-sensitive, urged her to move and she relaxed into him, shifting her hips in invitation.

It was all that he needed as he built the rhythm to boiling point with each thrust, rubbing her in places that were screaming out for more. Her fingernails dug into his back as she held onto her centre, a centre that was rapidly unwinding in her heightened state of arousal. She shut her eyes and pushed it back, wanting to feel him pound inside her for ever, to have his weight pressing her into the bed, to hear his groans in her ear.

But when he picked up the tempo she couldn't hold out any longer and everything unravelled in a shower of sparks and his own release joined hers, rocking it out together, calling each other's names until they lay spent and silent.

CHAPTER EIGHT

PATRICK'S HAND MOVED further up her leg as he nuzzled the skin just below Miranda's ear. His gut twisted into a hard knot of desire as a low, appreciative moan escaped her mouth. It was hard to believe it had been six months since they'd reconnected. Or that they'd been reduced to quietly necking on a couch on a Friday night in the dark like a pair of teenagers afraid of being sprung by their parents.

Or, in this case, *their children.*

Miranda shut her eyes against the sharp tug of desire. 'Patrick,' she warned, 'you're supposed to be going, remember?'

'Shh,' he murmured, his hand moving higher as he buzzed his lips down the curve of her neck.

Miranda's thighs fell apart of their own accord, her face turned towards his as the tug became more demanding. He kissed her eyes, her nose, her mouth and she wasn't even aware he was easing her backwards until her back hit soft cushions.

She pulled away from his mouth. 'Patrick,' she protested again, even weaker than the first time as his delicious weight settled between her thighs, his erection taunting her. 'The girls.'

'They're asleep,' he whispered, pleased now she was wearing the shirt that sat wide on her shoulders and low on her cleavage, the one she'd been deliberately taunting him with all evening.

Bending right in front of him to pick up something, giving him a bird's-eye view of her red satin bra with the overlay of black lace. The one he'd bought for her last month. With the matching underwear. Reaching across him at the dinner table, practically pushing her breasts in his face with that knowing smile.

The girls totally oblivious to the sexual undercurrent.

But as she extended her neck and his tongue swiped over her collar bone and continued lower, he was enjoying exacting his revenge.

'I don't think they are, yet,' she said, undulating her hips against his as his bristles prickled her throat, the delicious rasp rippling heat to the rest of her body.

Patrick licked lower as he eased his hand under her shirt, his palm finding and cupping the mound of satin and lace, his thumb brushing over the engorged tip he could feel through the fabric.

Miranda gasped and arched her back.

Patrick raised his head, seeking her mouth, when two little distant but distinct giggles could be heard.

His hand froze on her breast and for a moment neither of them moved. He dropped his forehead onto her chest, his breath rough, his pulse beating madly. It had been over a week since they'd been alone and he growled his frustration as Miranda pushed at his shoulders and they both moved reluctantly into an upright position.

He raked a hand through his hair, staring unseeingly at the flickering television, which was turned down too low to be heard over the roar of the pulse in his head.

'I think we should out ourselves.'

Miranda shook her head, also staring glumly at the TV. 'We agreed on a year.'

Patrick sighed. They had. They'd decided to give themselves twelve months, to take it slowly, to quietly get to know one another without the pressure of the outside world and its expectations. To be absolutely sure before breaking the idea to the girls. Too many relationships, particularly complicated ones, failed in the first year and Miranda was right, it was the sensible thing to do.

But the next six months stretched ahead interminably and after just *existing* for such a long time, he wanted more. He'd been good, noble and honourable—they both had. Putting their lives on hold. Doing the right thing. Didn't they deserve to be rewarded for that, to be happy, after years of putting everyone else first?

'I know we did. But that was before.'

Miranda glanced at him. 'Before what?'

'Before I realised I'm in love with you.'

He'd known it for a while but had only allowed it free rein tonight because frankly it had scared him witless. He'd never been in love before—not like this. Katie had been a wild infatuation, a roller-coaster of ups and downs, a constant state of anxiety.

Being with Miranda had been easy, so easy.

He hadn't realised love could be like that. That it could be gentle.

That something that filled you up so completely could be so easy.

He turned his head then and smiled at her. 'I love you, Miranda.'

Miranda gaped. For a crazy few seconds she actually thought she was having a stroke as his words completely paralysed her. He looked serious. Deadly serious. For someone like Patrick, who had been hurt so much by a woman already, who guarded his heart so fiercely, she'd figured such a declaration would be a long time in coming.

And she hadn't dared to ever let herself go there. The last six months she'd refused to give the L word any currency in her life. She and Patrick were simply enjoying each other, taking it easy. She'd deliberately banished it from her vocabulary.

'I…don't know what to say.'

Patrick cupped her face. '"I love you too" is customary.'

Miranda stood to remove herself from the temptation of Patrick all rumpled and in love with her. As he'd pointed out early on in their acquaintance, their relationship was complicated and she would do well to remember it.

'This is all a bit sudden,' she said, folding her arms across her chest because somehow he looked even sexier from this vantage point, his thighs spread in a blatantly male pose.

'No, it's not,' he said, capturing her gaze. 'I think I fell in love with you at the bar that night.'

Miranda's belly flopped. She often thought about that night. It had been such a charming interlude laced with a delightful sense of antici- pation. 'I'm not seventeen any more, Patrick. You don't need to tell me what you think I want to hear to get me into bed. In case you haven't no- ticed, that horse has already bolted.'

He grinned. 'I noticed.' She put her hands on her hips and he sobered. 'I'm not feeding you a line.' He sat forward, placing his elbows on his knees, his hands clasped loosely between them. 'I love you, Miranda. I think you love me too. Let's tell the world.'

Miranda wished now she wasn't standing as her knees started to wobble. Who'd have thought those three little words could mean so much to someone who was already more than a little jaded by love? She injected some iron into her stance.

Words were one thing, actions were another.

She needed all her i's dotted and t's crossed and the truth was, he wasn't free to make such a statement.

Miranda dropped her arms by her side. 'I'm not going to love a man who's married to someone else.'

'So…you do love me, you just…refuse to let yourself?'

Miranda knew it sounded crazy. 'I can't go there, Patrick.' She refused to think about the feelings that swirled and grew every time she saw him. 'I'm not going to be my mother. I'm not going to subject Lols to the ups and downs of that.'

Patrick reached for her unresisting hand. 'I wouldn't ever ask you to, Miranda. I hope you know that.' He squeezed her hand. 'The divorce should go through any day now.'

'I know. But…I can't…'

She couldn't allow herself to admit anything till then. She knew the divorce was a mere formality now but it was a mental hurdle for her, an important one. And just the touch of his hand was throwing everything into chaos, tempting her to walk around it instead of jumping over it clear and true with a free conscience.

'Not until after...'

Patrick tugged on her hand gently and pulled her into his lap, holding her close, her head tucked into his shoulder. 'It's fine,' he murmured.

Patrick understood how much it meant to her. How hard it was for her to be involved with a man who was still officially married. That she'd broken her cardinal rule to be with him.

The divorce had taken much longer to execute because of the peculiarities of his situation. Not being able to serve Katie with the papers due to her unknown whereabouts had muddied the waters but eventually, after jumping through all the legal hoops, including a court appearance, it was now just a matter of time.

'I'm sorry. I know you've done everything you could to get it through. And that it's been especially difficult given how hard it's been on Helen.'

Patrick stroked her arm absently. Helen had struggled with it. He knew it wasn't out of meanness or loss of control. It was just another link to her daughter being severed, the door finally closing.

'She'll get over it. Don't worry.'

Miranda hoped so. She'd only had three encounters with Patrick's mother-in-law since he'd started the divorce proceedings but they'd all been stilted and awkward.

They sat for a few minutes in the quiet darkness, Patrick's hand stroking up and down Miranda's bare arm. He'd never sat like this with Katie, and everything felt so right. Goose-bumps pebbled beneath the pads of his fingers and he inhaled the scent of her deep into his lungs with each stroke. She shifted against him and he shut his eyes as his body, already aroused from earlier, enjoyed the sensation.

Miranda, drifting in a heady splendour from his lazy touch, slowly became aware of his erection beneath her. She shifted against him as a pulse in her belly fluttered madly. 'Pervert,' she muttered.

He smiled to himself, enjoying the feel of her against him. 'Well, stop moving, then.'

Miranda smiled. 'It tickles.'

'What? This?' He thrust against her a little as his lips caressed her forehead.

Her smile broadened. That did, most definitely, *not* tickle. 'Your fingers,' she said, her voice thick in her throat.

He nuzzled her neck. 'I think the girls really are asleep now, you know.' He traced his tongue up her neck. 'God, you smell incredible,' he said, breathing her in until his head spun and his erection surged harder.

Miranda turned her head slightly to give him a little more of her neck for just a moment but suddenly his mouth was there and hers was on it and his tongue was invading and she was giving him access to all areas as she slipped her leg over his thigh to straddle him, and his hand slipped under the hem of her shirt.

She was practically putting up a red light and jiggling her butt right in front of him.

He *loved* her. *He loved her.*

'God, I want you,' he muttered against her mouth.

And it was like music to her ears. But…her conscience nagged her more.

It took Miranda a supreme effort to pull herself

back from that. *Supreme*. Her head was spinning, her heart was racing, her breasts were aching to be touched, her belly was melting into a puddle of lust.

He loved her.

But they couldn't. Their daughters were a room away. They had to be responsible.

Patrick looked at her, dazed, as his whole body screamed its displeasure. 'What?' he asked, breathing hard.

'Go!' She hauled herself off him, standing, stepping away, straightening her clothes. She pointed at the door. 'Go.'

Patrick could see by the ragged rise and fall of her chest how turned on she was despite the darkened room. Hell, he'd have been able to sense it had they been in the pitch blackness ten kilometres underground. 'Spoilsport.'

She gave him a grudging smile. 'Go.'

He rose from the lounge reluctantly and grinned when she moved even further away. 'So…getting back to my original proposal…once the divorce is through, I think we should tell the girls. I don't want to wait another six months. I don't want to wait any longer. I know what I want. And it's you.'

His hot autumn gaze blistered her with possession while his utter self-assurance oozed all over her like warmed maple syrup and whipped cream. 'Let's talk about it then,' she hedged.

She would *not* think about loving him, about altering their agreed-upon path, until after the D word.

He grinned. 'Spoken like a true mother.'

She smiled back and suddenly he was looking at her again not as a mother with responsibilities and sensibilities but as a woman whose clothes he could see right through! 'Stop that,' she chided as his gaze dropped to her nipples and they responded in kind.

He looked at her. 'I could help you with that…' his attention wandered to her nipples again before returning to her face '…situation.'

Miranda sucked in a breath. She was torn between laughing and ripping her shirt off and demanding he follow through with every wicked thought she could see in his golden-brown gaze.

'Leave. Now.'

He shrugged, holding up his hands in a surrender pose as he walked slowly backwards. 'Just sayin'.'

She grinned. 'Noted.'

Patrick felt the door against his back and wanted to leave about as much as he wanted to drill a hole in his head. He was so turned on right now he doubted he'd even be able to see the road properly even though he could see her erect nipples in the dark and way across the room.

'Call me during the night if they…become too much of a nuisance.'

She sent him a faux mortified look. 'I will be sleeping soundly, you scoundrel.'

He grinned. 'I don't know about you, but I'm not going to sleep a wink.'

And then he turned and left because a man was only blessed with so much self-control and he'd reached his limit for the day.

Miranda smiled as he left, her heart filling up with giddiness again, which she determinedly ignored. For now she was happy and she wasn't going to analyse that!

Which lasted all of about five minutes.

She checked on the girls and discovered that

while they were, indeed, finally asleep, Bud mark six was also doing a very good impression of sleep in his little bowl.

Too good.

Miranda looked down at the fish floating lifelessly on his side. The same fish that had, only an hour ago, been frolicking around like a spring lamb, causing the girls to giggle like loons.

Maybe he'd been having a seizure. And drowned.

'Oh, Bud,' she whispered, picking up the round bowl and staring at him through the thick glass. 'Not again!'

Thank God Kevin from the pet shop played a Friday night poker game with his geek buddies in the back of the shop. She shook her head as she dialled his number—she shouldn't know so much about the habits of a middle-aged pet-shop owner.

After assuring her he'd be there if she wanted to pop down for Bud mark seven, Miranda had no choice but to ring the one guy she needed to stay away from. Nan was out on a pensioner trip to the granite belt wine district and couldn't be called on to come and sit with the girls.

That left her no choice unless she wanted to deal with two distraught five-year-olds in the morning.

Patrick smiled at the screen of his phone as he climbed out of his car, a tiny thrill of anticipation buzzing through his system. He leaned against the door as he answered it. 'You want me to talk dirty to you?'

Miranda laughed, her toes curling at the deliciously sexy edge to his voice. And if she hadn't been holding a bowl containing the body of the dearly departed Bud, she may well have gone with a little phone sex. 'No. But I do need a favour.'

'You want me to come around and deal with it in person?'

'Behave,' she warned, but her voice was a little too husky to be taken seriously. 'Are you home yet?'

Patrick grinned. 'Just pulled in.'

Miranda sighed. 'Darn.'

'What?' Patrick straightened as he clued in to the note of strain in her voice. 'Is something wrong?'

'Bud died.'

It took Patrick a moment to compute what she was saying and he relaxed back against the car. 'Poor Bud. Although I'm not surprised. Bud needs a girl. Sexual frustration is a killer. I ought to know.'

Miranda smiled despite the situation. 'Will you be serious?'

'I am very serious about sexual frustration.'

Miranda decided it was best to ignore him. 'I'm sorry, I know you're home but can you go to the pet shop and pick up a new Bud and bring him back? Nan's away so I can't leave.'

Patrick checked his watch. 'It's ten-thirty at night. The pet shop is open?'

'Kevin's there, he knows what I need.'

'What on earth is he doing at work at a *pet shop* at this hour of night? Does Kevin not have a life?'

'Poker game.' There was silence for a long moment. 'I know, it's sad that I know that. Will you please just do it?'

Not one to look a gift horse in the mouth, Patrick said, 'You owe me.'

The low, suggestive note slipped down her

spine and Miranda gripped the phone. 'I'll text you the address.'

And she hung up before she offered to let him have a pound of flesh—gentleman's choice—in exchange for door-to-door delivery.

An hour later he was back, toting a water-filled plastic bag with two fish and a grin the size of the Great Australian Bight.

'Bud seems to have cloned,' she said as he produced the bag.

'At least someone's going to get lucky tonight.'

She took it from him, careful to not touch his fingers. He was still in the same clothes as earlier and if anything his coming to her rescue had ramped up his sexiness to lethal proportions. If anyone had said before tonight that a man bearing two girly looking goldfish could look hot, she'd have laughed.

And yet here he was, standing in her home. Oozing hotness.

'And how are we going to explain the second fish?' she enquired as she tipped them into their new home.

'We'll tell them Bud had a baby.'

Miranda raised an eyebrow. 'Oh, you want to have the *baby* talk with them, do you?'

Patrick faltered as a bunch of potential complications arose. He rubbed his jaw. 'Hmm. Good point. Tell them the mermaids decided Bud needed a girlfriend.'

Miranda's arms broke out in goose-bumps at the delicious rasp of his whiskers. They were standing side by side at the kitchen bench, looking down into the bowl with two fish that certainly didn't look like they were about to go steady any time soon. They were definitely keeping their distance.

His arm brushed against hers. The heat from his thighs radiated her way. She could see his pursed lips in her peripheral vision.

Miranda picked up the bowl, determined to be strong. To step away from temptation. *Well away.* 'I think,' she said, heading for Lola's room, 'just mentioning mermaids will be sufficient deflection. Good thinking.'

Patrick followed her and the enticing swing of her hips in her regulation jeans. They walked past her bedroom to Lola's room and he hung back in the doorway as Miranda quietly placed the bowl back on the table that usually nestled between the two beds but which tonight was pushed to the side to make way for the princess cubby house he'd helped them construct for their sleeping pleasure.

She snapped off the lamp she'd thrown a pink silky scarf over, instantly dousing the low pink light. He watched Miranda as she carefully picked her way out of the room and joined him by the door. They both gazed down at the sleeping faces of their daughters. They lay beside each other, their hands intertwined, their little bow mouths slack, their breathing deep and even.

'They're so beautiful,' Patrick whispered as his heart squeezed at their obvious affection for each other.

Miranda nodded on a rush of love for Ruby as well as Lola. 'Yes.'

Patrick put his arm around her shoulder and almost sighed when she snuggled into his side.

'Thank you,' Miranda said after a while. 'For coming to the rescue.'

He didn't say anything for a moment as they gazed at the girls. 'It's my job,' he murmured. 'I'm the daddy.'

Miranda let it wash over her. It would be nice to have a man around. Someone to take out the rubbish, check cupboards for monsters, replace dead fish in the middle of the night.

To lie with. To hold. To cherish.

She shut her eyes against the seduction of it all then she pulled away. If she didn't let go now, she might not let go at all.

Patrick followed her, the need to touch her, kiss her growing by the second, and as they drew level with her bedroom it took over. He captured her arm and she turned to face him, blinking up at him all wide-eyed and gorgeous in that infernal blouse, which was nothing but a barrier to the satin, lace and skin he knew lay beneath.

'Patrick.'

If it had been stern or laden with reproach it would have stopped him in his tracks but it had a throaty kind of desperation to it that ramped up his desire. His hand slid to her cheek, cupping it. 'Now…about that payment,' he said, as he dropped his head to savour the taste of her mouth.

She shivered and moaned a little and moved closer, and it was all the encouragement he needed. He walked her backwards until they were in the privacy of her bedroom.

Miranda dragged her mouth away. 'You should go, Patrick,' she said, trying to convince herself as much as him as she stared at his mouth.

Patrick tried to drag his rampant body under control. To slow his heart rate, to even his breath. 'I know,' he said. 'I know. I just…' He brushed her fringe off her face. 'I love you,' he murmured.

Miranda shut her eyes as his words stroked every erogenous zone she had. 'Don't say that,' she begged.

'Why not?' he asked as she opened her eyes. 'I love you, I love you. I love you, I love you.'

Miranda rocked her head from side to side as her belly tightened, her breasts burgeoned, her fingers itched. Those three little words were the ultimate in foreplay. 'Stop,' she said desperately as her body melted into a puddle.

Patrick smiled triumphantly as her pupils dilated. 'Ah, I see,' he murmured. Very slowly he dropped a kiss behind her ear. 'I love you.' And then another on the underside of her jaw. 'I love you.' And one further down where a pulse fluttered madly in her throat. 'I love you.'

'Okay,' she breathed out in ragged surrender as he stroked his tongue along her collar bone.

He lifted his head and smiled, his mouth hovering a fraction from hers. 'Okay, what?'

Miranda shivered as his lips whispered the words over hers. 'You have to go home straight after.'

Patrick smiled.

Then he kissed her deep and hard and hungry and neither of them spoke for a very long time.

CHAPTER NINE

PATRICK HALF STIRRED as early light filtered through the lacy curtains and tried to remember the last time he'd woken up with such a feeling of contentment. Miranda was warm and relaxed all spooned up against him and he allowed himself the luxury of lazily nuzzling along her neck and shoulder.

The pleasant feeling unfortunately did not last for long as he came more awake and other things filtered in. Like loud whispering coming from the end of the bed. His heart started to beat a little harder as the implication of that sank in. He peeked up and found himself looking into two sets of curious eyes—one china blue, the other emerald green.

Holy crap! The bedside clock said almost six. *He was supposed to have left hours ago!*

He turned his face to Miranda and whispered in her ear, 'Wake up, we've been sprung.'

Miranda came out of her sexually charged drowse into instant consciousness, her eyes flying open, the light filling her room slapping her in the face with a mega-dose of reality. She scrambled to a sitting position, taking the sheet with her. They both did, sitting back against the bedhead, facing their interested audience with the sheet pulled up to cover their state of undress.

Lola, holding her goldfish bowl, recovered first. *Naturally.*

'How come you're in my mummy's bed?' she asked Patrick.

'Well…' He slid a sideways look at Miranda as he cleared his throat.

Miranda jumped in. 'Patrick was too tired to go home last night so he slept here instead.' She held her breath. Lola generally took explanations at face value, too wrapped up in her own world to dig too deeply into anything that didn't have an immediate bearing on it.

Ruby was a different prospect. Miranda could see her green eyes assessing the situation a little more closely. She chewed on her lip with her two new front teeth, which had finally arrived a few weeks ago. 'You could have thlept with me, Daddy.'

Patrick forced his best daddy grin on his face. 'You two were hogging the bed,' he protested lightly. 'There wasn't any room for me and my big feet.' And then, deciding the best defence was offence, he said, 'You're up early, Rubyloo. Were the beg bugs biting?'

Lola giggled. 'No, silly.' She held up her gold-fish bowl. 'Something...*magical*...' she breathed the word out, garnishing it with a brand of reverence only a five-year-old girl could '...has happened.'

Miranda took in the two fish, still apparently not the best of chums, and plastered the biggest look of surprise on her face she'd ever faked. 'Wow! Two fish? But...' she spread her hands dramatically, '...how'd that happen?'

Both little girls shook their heads. 'Ith a miracle,' Ruby whispered, her eyes large.

Patrick shook his head. 'It's the mermaids, I reckon.'

'Mermaids?' Lola squeaked.

'I reckon they knew that Bud was lonely and sent him a friend.'

'Really, Daddy?' Ruby asked, her voice hushed, her eyes glowing with excitement.

He nodded. 'I think so.'

'But...' Lola frowned at Ruby '...we didn't see a mermaid.'

Ruby's face fell as she looked at her friend. 'No,' she agreed. And then they both looked at the adults for an explanation.

'Mermaids are like the tooth fairy, right, Miranda?' Patrick said, getting into the groove of the fantasy.

'Right,' Miranda agreed, her heart still fluttering madly at the situation they were in. And shouldn't be.

'You never see them, they come when you're asleep. But they visit fish at night. *All* the time.'

Miranda dug her finger discreetly into his leg. He'd made up enough for one day. Embellishment was a bad idea—always keep it simple. She made a mental note to tell their teacher about the mermaid story, which would surely come up next week at school.

Both girls were looking at him expectantly for more but Patrick wisely heeded Miranda's prompt. 'Who feels like pancakes?' he asked.

'Yay!' Both girls cheered in unison.

Patrick breathed a sigh of relief over how easily distracted five-year-olds were. 'Well, go on and feed the fish and get dressed, and we'll meet you in the kitchen in five minutes,' he announced.

Miranda watched the girls hurry to the door, half of her grateful for their hasty exit, the other half worrying that the fish were about to be displaced from their bowl with each tsunami-like wave of the water. Lola stopped abruptly and turned at the entrance, the water sloshing precariously, fish still in situ.

She looked at her mother, her gaze suddenly shrewd. 'Why aren't you wearing your pyjamas?'

Patrick heard the little strangled gurgle at the back of Miranda's throat as she stared blankly at her daughter. He bit the side of his cheek. He shouldn't laugh, it wasn't funny. He had a pretty good idea that Miranda was going to be distinctly annoyed. But she looked very cute when she was flummoxed.

'I was…hot,' Miranda said lamely.

Lola rolled her eyes. 'You should have turned the fan on, Mummy.' And then she shimmied out of the room after Ruby.

Miranda let out a breath as her daughter's blonde curls finally disappeared from view, and she dropped her forehead into her palms.

Patrick's chuckle surrounded her as he said, 'You should see your face.'

Miranda's head snapped up. 'You,' she said, pushing his arm, 'were supposed to leave. That was the deal.'

'Hey,' he half laughed, half protested. 'I had every intention. I must have just drifted off...'

Miranda flicked the sheet aside and slid out of bed. 'This is bad,' she muttered as she picked up her discarded bra and undies off the floor.

Patrick watched her climb into her underwear, admiring her as she wrapped all her fineness in red satin and black lace. 'It'll be fine.'

Miranda shot him a thunderous look. 'Well, don't just lie there—we have pancakes to make. And some damage control to do.'

'Ah...yeah...I'm going to need a minute.' He grimaced.

As it turned out, there wasn't really any need for damage control. The girls helped Patrick make the pancakes and they all sat around the table, eating them as if Ruby and Lola sprang them naked in bed together every morning.

Which, of course, they probably would should they take the relationship to the next stage.

Miranda shivered at the thought because sitting here amidst the cosy domesticity of Saturday morning breakfast, Lola chatting away ten to the dozen, she wanted that. Her heart ached for it so badly she could barely breathe every time she looked at Patrick and Lola interacting.

This was what she wanted.

What she'd always wanted her entire life. A family. A true working unit. A mum and a dad and two children living in a gingerbread house in an enchanted forest.

Well, maybe not quite…but definitely not what she'd had. A single mother, an absent, resentful father, a dysfunctional household.

Maybe Patrick was right. Maybe they could have it sooner rather than later. She glanced at him and he chose that moment to look her way in his rumpled clothes from yesterday and smile, and she drew in a deep shuddery breath at the enormity of it. She smiled back.

'Are you going to be my mummy?'

Startled by the comment, Miranda dragged her gaze off Patrick and onto his daughter. Ruby may have been five but she was an intuitive little thing. Unlike Lola, she was very in tune with people's emotions, sensitive to undercurrents. She glanced at Patrick and he gave a slight shrug.

'What…makes you say that, Ruby?' she hedged, noticing that Lola had stopped chatting and was now listening intently.

'Jamie Biddle theth his daddy hugth his mummy in bed a lot.'

'That's not the only criterion to being a mummy,' Miranda said tentatively.

'He theth they thmile at each other a lot too.'

Patrick suppressed the quick grin that rose to his lips by pressing them together. 'How would you feel about that, Ruby-loo?' he asked, casually ignoring Miranda's frown in his peripheral vision. 'About Miranda being your mummy?'

Ruby put her arms on the table and balanced her chin on sticky, maple-syrup palms. She looked adorable as her brows drew together in fierce concentration. 'I already have a mummy.'

'Yes, you do,' Miranda said, jumping in

quickly. Maybe Katie didn't deserve to be part of her daughter's life, running away as she had and not coming back, but, being a mother herself and the child of an aloof mother, Miranda felt some sympathy for Katie.

And she never wanted Ruby to feel torn.

'And she will always be your mummy.'

'But we…' Patrick indicated them all by swizzling his finger around in the air between them '…could all still become a family.'

'Patrick,' Miranda murmured.

Her eyes had narrowed and she shook her head at him almost imperceptibly, but Patrick wasn't dissuaded. He knew she wasn't ready for this to be discussed but sometimes there were openings that were too good to ignore.

Ruby's eyes opened wide.

Patrick ignored Miranda's disapproval. 'Miranda could be like a…second mummy.'

'And you could be my daddy?' Lola interjected, cottoning on quickly to what was in it for her. Having never really had a daddy to begin with, Lola had obviously decided that *numero uno* spot was his for the taking.

Patrick felt the innocent question sock him

right between the eyes. He'd always imagined himself with three or four kids but when Katie had run out on him, just getting through the day had taken up all his energy—there had been no time for happy family daydreams. Suddenly he felt like that was back in play. 'If you like.'

Ruby regarded him with solemn eyes. 'What about Grandma? Grandma would thill live with uth?'

Even though Miranda hated the prematurity of this discussion—there was a knot in her stomach as big as a football—she couldn't bear the uncertainty in Ruby's sweet little voice. 'Absolutely,' she said, her voice firm, her smile genuine. 'Grandmothers are the most important part of families, aren't they, Lols?'

Lola nodded solemnly but her busy brain was already thinking way ahead. She put her arm around Ruby's shoulder. 'When you get married, could we be flower girls?'

Miranda stood abruptly. *Okay, enough now.* They were tempting fate and she didn't want it to go any further. 'All right, now, let's not get ahead of ourselves.' She started gathering dishes. 'We'll think about this all again at Christmas time. You girls need to go and wash your hands,' she said briskly.

The girls slipped out of their seats without protest, seemingly unconcerned about the deep and meaningful issues that had just been discussed. 'Come on, Rubes, let's go and practise our flower-girl walk,' Lola said as they scampered away.

Miranda let the dishes clatter to the table as she watched them skip away. She turned on him, hands shoved on hips, temper simmering. 'You've created a monster.'

Patrick shrugged. 'There was an opening. I was just testing the water.'

'They're practising their flower-girl walk,' she hissed.

He grinned. He knew she was mad but maybe this hadn't been such a bad thing. 'So let's not disappoint them. Let's move in together.'

Miranda gaped at him. 'Are you crazy? That is not what we discussed.'

They'd discussed dating openly for a period of time and then when Ruby and Lola were used to that they'd start spending nights at each other's houses with the girls in tow.

'We need to slow it down.'

Patrick wasn't so sure after last night. He was beginning to think they should be doing the opposite. He finally knew what he wanted and she was standing right in front of him. He walked round her side of the table, pulled her, resisting all the way, into his arms. 'Maybe we need to speed it up.'

Then he kissed her deep and hard.

By the time Miranda broke away she was breathing heavily, and scraping her thoughts back together proved to be a task almost beyond her. She flopped onto the chair behind her, her knees not quite as strong as she'd like.

'So much could go wrong,' she said, looking up at him.

Patrick could see the plea in her smoky green eyes as she begged him to understand.

'We don't have a normal situation,' she continued. 'And I've rushed headlong into something before and Lola suffered the consequences.'

Patrick sank into the chair next to her, his thighs bracketing the outside of hers as he reached for her hand. 'What we have is not like that, Miranda. I know it's scary but we can't be afraid to be happy because things haven't worked in the past.'

Miranda nodded because she knew he was telling the truth. 'I'm not saying we shouldn't do it,' she said. 'I just don't think we should rush.'

Patrick frowned because her hand shook and her voice trembled. She seemed so...scared. 'What are you afraid is going to happen?' he asked.

Miranda's biggest fear loomed in her mind and instead of pushing it away like she had for the last six months she gave it voice. 'I'm afraid Katie will come back and throw everything into chaos.'

Patrick blinked, taken aback by the revelation. 'Waiting won't change that,' he said. 'That can happen any time.'

Miranda nodded. It wasn't what she wanted to hear but it was true nonetheless. 'I know.'

What she wanted to hear was him saying that by hook or by crook he wouldn't allow her anywhere near them. Sometimes the memories of her childhood, of her mother pining for a man who had divided loyalties, were still very powerful. She didn't want to be in that situation.

But she was torn. She didn't have the right to keep Ruby's biological mother out of Ruby's life and the part of her that was a mother didn't want to either.

Patrick slid his hand along her jaw, cupping it, raising her face until she was looking at him. 'Are you…? Do you think I'm still in love with her?'

Miranda shook her head because he'd told her he wasn't and she believed him. 'I just don't think you fully appreciate how difficult blending families can be. How much strain it can put on a relationship.'

'Hey.' He stroked his thumb along her cheekbone. 'Who's getting ahead of herself now? Why don't we cross that bridge if and when we get to it?'

'I know.' She gave him a small smile. 'Sorry. Put it down to the whole daughter-of-a-homewrecker paranoia.'

Patrick didn't realise until this moment just how much Miranda's upbringing had scarred her. 'You and Ruby and Lola will always come first for me, and if Katie ever does show up again and wants to cause trouble then I will fight tooth and nail to keep this family together. I will protect that with my life.'

A huge lump blocked Miranda's throat and tears stung her eyes. 'I know,' she whispered.

Patrick smiled. 'Now can we speed this thing up a little?'

Miranda rolled her eyes and pulled back from him. 'We'll talk about it. After the divorce.'

Patrick leaned back in his chair. 'Okay. But you know I'm not going to take no for an answer, right?'

She snorted. 'Yeah, I figured.'

He sobered again, leaning forward and reaching for her hand. 'It's going to be fine, Miranda. I promise. I know you've lived cautiously for the last few years, we both have, but, trust me, it's going to work out for us.'

Miranda smiled as she linked her fingers with his. 'I'm going to hold you to that.'

And for three days Miranda actually believed that he was right. That things were going to work out. They were expecting the official divorce papers to arrive this week and then, maybe then, she'd feel like things were more set in stone. For someone who had lived a lot of her life under the cloud of uncertainty, stone was a good thing.

Then whammy number one hit.

She was working the emergency theatre on Tuesday afternoon when she went to the entrance to accept her next patient. The anaesthetic nurse always took handover from the ward nurse, asking the patient a lot of questions they'd already been asked at least a dozen times. She then accompanied the patient to the anaesthetic room, where they went through the same questions again.

Miranda knew it frustrated patients but it was better to go through the same things over and over than to wake up with an amputated right leg instead of the intended left one.

Her patient that afternoon was a man who'd been involved in a jet-ski accident on the Brisbane River. He'd sustained a badly fractured humerus close to the elbow joint that required pinning and plating.

The emergency room nurse smiled at her and handed her a chart as they exchanged some brief pleasantries. Miranda said a brief hello to her patient before signalling her colleague to begin the handover. 'This is twenty-four-year-old Mal Anderson who—'

Miranda didn't hear the rest as she frowned down at the chart with the familiar name. It took a couple of seconds to compute. *Oh, my God!*

'Mal?' She looked down at her patient properly. His golden curls were obscured by the theatre cap all patients had foisted on them for their stint in the operating theatre, but his bronzed face looked as carefree as it always had.

He blinked up at her for a moment, his forehead crinkled then she watched realisation slowly dawn. 'Mirry?'

Miranda didn't know what to say. She'd known things had been going too smoothly to be true but never in a million years had running into *Lola's* father popped up as a possibility. She'd been convinced Katie would be the fly in the ointment.

He smiled at her, the same toothpaste-ad smile he'd flashed her six years ago that had made her feel special, the centre of attention, and his eyes still startlingly blue. For a moment she could see Lola in him so clearly it almost stole her breath.

But his ugly words came back to her, negating all his blond good looks, and his presence at this time in her life just made her jittery. Wary and vulnerable.

'Oh, my God,' he said. 'How are you?'

Conscious of her audience, Miranda gave him a noncommittal 'Fine' before excusing herself to get back to the handover. When it was done she plastered a smile on her face, nodded at the orderly to wheel the trolley and asked Mal what he'd been up to.

By the time they reached the anaesthetic room and Mal was wheeled into position a minute later it was plain he was still chasing waves. But he'd gone global, getting himself a job as a photographer on a famous surfing magazine.

She remembered that he'd always been taking pictures. That he'd taken a bunch of her. That she had them in an old box somewhere. She hadn't thought about them in years.

'What are you doing in Brisbane?' she asked.

'There's a carnival at Surfer's Paradise starting tomorrow. Although...' he grimaced '...I don't know how good my trigger finger is going to be.'

She looked at his arm, which was in a sling. 'That could be a problem.'

'What about you?' he asked. 'I didn't know you wanted to be a nurse.'

It was on the tip of her tongue to tell him he'd never asked but that was a little unfair. Her career prospects hadn't exactly come up during their three weeks of sun, surf and sex. Her only objective had been to be with someone who *wanted* her. For a change. He might not have asked but that had more than suited her too.

'Yep. Always,' she said evasively, turning to the bench. 'The anaesthetist should be here shortly,' she said as she checked the drugs and equipment were ready.

There was silence for a moment or two which he broke.

'I'm sorry. I owe you an apology for the way I acted...the things I said on the phone that day.'

Miranda straightened her shoulders. 'It's fine,' she dismissed.

'No. I was in a state of shock and I panicked but that doesn't excuse it.'

Miranda turned back to face to him. 'You weren't alone.'

'Did you...did you have the baby?'

Miranda contemplated lying to him. It might

be easier and kinder in the long run. And maybe he wanted her to lie to him? It would be so easy. She could tell him she'd had a termination. Or a miscarriage. And he wouldn't be any the wiser. But the same sense of rightness and fairness that had driven her to ring and tell him about Lola all those years ago wasn't going to let her go rogue now.

He had a right to know he had a child.

His other rights didn't even bear thinking about. 'Yes.'

She was aware it wasn't exactly the time or place to be giving him such news. She'd seen on his chart that he'd had some morphine half an hour ago but he'd asked the question and, under the influence of drugs or not, he deserved the truth.

Mal lifted his head off the pillow and looked at her. 'So...I'm a father?'

Miranda nodded. 'Yes. A little girl. Lola.' She drummed her fingers against the bench. 'She looks like you.'

His head fell back onto the pillow. 'A little girl. I have a little girl.' He shut his eyes and rocked his head gently from side to side before opening them again and saying to the ceiling, 'I'm a daddy.'

Miranda frowned. *No.* Patrick was a daddy. Mal was a...*sperm donor.*

He looked up again. 'She must be, what?' He squinted for a moment. 'Five...six?'

'Five.'

'Have you got a picture of her?'

Miranda shook her head. 'Not on me, no.'

The swing door was pushed open and suddenly Miranda's day got a little bit worse as Patrick strode in, smiling.

'Bob's case has run over so I'm going to do this,' he informed her chirpily. 'Hi,' he said to the patient on the trolley, extending his hand. 'I'm Patrick Costello and I'll be doing your anaesthetic today.'

'This is Mal. Mal Anderson,' Miranda said.

Patrick thought the name seemed familiar but he was preoccupied by the goofy look on the guy's face. He'd have thought there would be a lot of pain considering the X-rays he'd just seen of the rather nasty fracture. 'I think you've met Mr Morphine,' he joked with Mal.

'Nah,' Mal said. 'I just found out I've got a kid.' He grinned.

Miranda suppressed the urge to tell him he'd always known that but Mal was on a roll. 'Lola. Her name's Lola.' He raised his head off the bed and looked at Miranda standing frozen at the bench. 'Isn't that right, Mirry?'

It took a moment for Patrick to catch up. He frowned at the overly bronzed, fit-looking guy on the trolley then looked at Miranda, who looked even paler than she usually did.

Like she'd seen a ghost.

'This is Mal,' she said through stiff lips. 'Lola's father.'

Patrick stared at her for a moment as that particular piece of news filtered in.

Holy crap.

CHAPTER TEN

A FEW HOURS later Patrick and Miranda were sitting at a fast-food restaurant, absently watching the girls play on the playground equipment through the big glass windows. They sucked on thick shakes as they adjusted to the unexpected development.

'It's going to be fine,' Patrick said, placing his hand over hers and giving it a squeeze. He'd said it at least a dozen times now but Miranda didn't look any more convinced.

Miranda nodded absently and hoped he was right. But she had a bad feeling in the pit of her stomach and maybe that was her natural pessimistic tendency due to the entrenched disappointments of her childhood but, regardless, she couldn't shake it.

She looked at Patrick. 'What if he wants to see her?'

Patrick placed his drink on the table. 'I don't think you should get ahead of yourself.'

'She never even asks me about her father. She just accepts that some kids have one parent and that's that.'

'You do know she will, though, right? One day?'

Miranda heard a note of something she couldn't put her finger on in his voice. Reproach? She glared at him. 'What's that supposed to mean?' she snapped.

Patrick sighed. 'Nothing... Miranda, I—'

'What, Patrick? Just say it.'

'Girls need fathers too, that's all.'

'Well, isn't that what you're going to be?' she demanded, knowing her voice was sounding shrill but somehow unable to stop. 'Do you want to share her with him? A virtual stranger who'll flit in and out of her life and never be there for her?'

Just like her own father.

'It's not ideal, Miranda, granted, but that's the reality of our situation.'

'Reality sucks.'

Patrick smiled. He couldn't argue with that one. 'That it does.'

Miranda couldn't believe how calm he was being. It was reassuring, she supposed, but also a little disconcerting. 'So you're not worried about this at all?'

Patrick shook his head. 'The only thing that would worry me is if you still carrying some kind of flame for him.'

Miranda looked at him askance but it was a legitimate concern. 'Don't looked so shocked,' he said. 'He's a good-looking guy. He's certainly closer to your age than I am and shared histories can be a seductive thing. Especially when there's a very tangible link connecting you.'

'Don't be ridiculous,' she dismissed. 'Mal was just a…a fling, a symptom of loneliness and lack of attention. I never felt anything for him other than teenage hormones and desperation.'

'You didn't ever imagine yourself just a little in love with him?'

Miranda shook her head vehemently. 'Never.'

Patrick knew he shouldn't smile but he did anyway. It was good to hear her instant rejection. 'Well, that's good to know.'

Miranda rolled her eyes at his smug grin. 'This is not an ego-stroking exercise,' she said. It was supposed to be stern but she found herself smiling at him in return. 'This is *serious*,' she went on, pulling herself back in line. 'You must have *some* opinion.'

'Okay, fine,' he said, sitting up straighter. 'You want me to be serious, to have an opinion? Fine. But I can't do this from some great sensible emotional distance. I'm a father too and it would *kill* me to not be able to see Ruby grow up—'

'But yours is a different situation,' Miranda interrupted.

'I know. But all I can tell you is what I think and feel from a father's point of view. I would want to be part of Ruby's life. And the facts are that as Lola's biological father, he has rights—' he held up his hand as Miranda tried to interject again '—despite not wanting anything to do with her at the beginning. None of which matters because it'll probably not even come to that so I don't think we should waste any energy worrying about it.'

Miranda knew he was right but his calmness drove her nuts. For years she'd wondered if she'd have her own family one day, she and Lola, one that was good and solid and worked and nothing like the complicated disaster that she'd grown up in. And finally she'd let down her guard enough to think that it was within reach and suddenly it was complicated again.

'Cross that bridge if we get to it?' she said.

'Exactly.'

Lola ran past the window with Ruby in tow and Miranda watched them on the slippery slide for a moment or two. She looked back at Patrick, his olive complexion and autumn eyes so much a part of her already she found it hard to breathe. She wanted this so much. Him and her. Lola and Ruby.

Surely the universe wouldn't be so cruel as to snatch it all away?

She smiled at him. 'Of course. I'm sorry. I've got my knickers in a bit of a twist, haven't I?'

Patrick grinned. 'Always willing to help a lady untwist her knickers. That's my specialty.'

Miranda shook her head at him. '*You're* twisted.'

His chuckle reached deep inside her and squeezed.

* * *

Despite Patrick's conviction that all would be fine, Miranda didn't have a very good sleep. She kept thinking about Patrick's mention of Mal's *rights*.

Frankly, she didn't care a jot about his rights. She only cared about her daughter. She didn't want to keep Lola from her father but she did want to be able to control the circumstances as much as possible, to ease the transition.

And somehow she'd just always assumed it was something that she wouldn't have to worry about until Lola was a teenager and questions of identity were the norm.

Eventually exhaustion won out and she dropped off in the small hours. Miranda knew she wasn't going to relax fully now until Mal had moved on. Well on.

Maybe she'd never really relax again.

The next morning her fear ratcheted up another notch. She got a message mid-morning to say that a Mal Anderson had left a message asking her to come and see him on the ortho ward. By the time lunchtime came around the ward clerk had handed her three more messages from him.

Patrick watched her thumb through the written messages with a look of trepidation on her face. 'Best to get it over with, don't you think?' he asked, as he sidled up to her in the tearoom.

Miranda looked up from the note in her hand, absently trying to guess the intent behind them. 'I suppose...'

He put his arm around her shoulder, uncaring for once that Lilly was watching them like a hawk. 'Do you want me to come with you?'

Miranda desperately wanted to say yes. But she'd been fighting her own battles for a long time and she wasn't going to surrender that control now, no matter how appealing it was to lean on someone else for once. 'No, I'll be fine.'

She gave him what she hoped was a reassuring smile, although she doubted it even registered on her face. 'I'll go up now and see him in my break,' she said, tucking the messages in her scrub pocket.

Patrick watched her leave and part of him wanted to catch up and tell her he was coming regardless but he knew her and Mal needed to have a frank and open conversation about Lola and his presence would only serve to stifle it.

So he turned away, catching Lilly's triumphant gaze as he did so.

Miranda dressed in her civvies and was up on the ward within five minutes. Mal had one of the private rooms and he was watching a sports channel on the television when she entered. His injured arm was elevated in a sling and he quickly flicked off the television with the remote resting in his good hand when she said, 'Hi.'

Mal smiled at her. 'Thanks for coming.'

'No worries,' Miranda murmured. 'How's the arm?'

'Good.' He nodded. 'Doc reckons I can go home tomorrow.'

'That's good. Excellent… Much pain?'

'A little. They have some good drugs here, though.' He laughed but sobered quickly when he realised Miranda wasn't laughing. 'Sorry, bad joke.' He grimaced. 'Sit down.'

He indicated the chair beside his bed and Miranda wished her legs were strong enough to refuse, but they were trembling so hard she wasn't sure how much longer they were going to hold her upright. She sank into it gratefully.

'You must hate me,' Mal said.

Miranda blinked at the bald statement. His words had hurt but a part of her had understood how crazy fear made a person.

'No. I don't hate you.'

'I was…terrified.'

She'd been pretty terrified herself. 'It's okay. I understand. Really. It was a lot to deal with.'

'But *you* dealt with it.'

Miranda shrugged. 'It was my choice.'

There was silence for a moment then Miranda remembered the photo she'd taken from her wallet on impulse before she'd shut her locker. She fished it out of her back pocket.

'Here.' She passed him a picture of Lola sliding down a slippery dip, her fingers shaking. 'This is Lola. It was taken at school last month.'

Mal inspected the photo. 'Wow. She *does* look like me.'

Miranda nodded. 'No DNA tests required,' she said, her voice brittle.

Mal looked at her sharply. 'I didn't ask to see you to cause trouble, Mirry.'

'Why did you, then?'

Mal looked down at the photo, ran his thumb over his daughter's face. 'I'd like to see her.'

His quiet request slammed into Miranda with all the power of a tornado and for a moment the whole world stopped. She could hear the beat of her heart, the suck of her breath both loud in her ears. Her skin prickled as if someone was jabbing a thousand needles into her.

This was what she'd feared.

'Miranda?'

Mal's voice dragged Miranda back from the pit of despair into which she'd been sinking. She blinked at him as she gathered her thoughts. She knew she had to be very careful how she handled this now. The temptation to get up and yell and scream and be dramatic, like her mother used to whenever she was discussing Miranda with her father, was surprisingly strong.

But she wasn't her mother and she wanted Mal on her side, willing to work towards what was best for Lola, not angry and working against her.

She chose her words carefully, looking at her hands as she clasped them together to stop the trembling. 'It's your right to see her so I'm not going to say that you can't.'

She looked at him then because she really wanted him to understand what she was saying.

'But I am going to ask you not to. For now. If you want to be in her life, you need to be *in her life*, Mal. Solid, stable, reliable. Here. Not someone like my father who was never there for me. Lola needs to know that *she* is the most important thing to you, not some wave somewhere.'

Miranda paused to let her words sink in. She'd spent hours spewing out all her father issues to him and he'd been a good listener. He knew how her father's neglect had scarred her.

'There's going to come a time in her life when she's going to want to know you and I won't stop her, but I'd really rather that was led by *her* and *her* desire to connect with you rather than the other way around. Let's face it, if we hadn't had this chance meeting you'd still be oblivious to her existence so I'm asking you to put *her* first. Let *her* come to you.'

Miranda finished, hoping that she'd been clear. That she'd appealed to his common human decency. A lot was riding on her words.

Mal stared at the photo for a long time then nodded absently. 'You're right,' he murmured. He had a great life he didn't want to surrender. Not yet. 'I'm sorry, I just… You're right.' He gave a half-smile as he passed the picture back. 'I guess I'm a little too itinerant at the moment.'

Miranda almost collapsed in on herself as relief swamped her like a torrential downpour. 'Keep it,' she said, smiling for the first time since she'd entered the room.

She had dozens more and the real thing to look at, to squeeze tight every day.

She placed her hand on his. 'Thank you,' she said. 'This means…everything to me.'

Mal smiled. 'I should at least help financially.'

Miranda shook her head. 'Oh, no. I'm fine. We're doing fine.' They might not be living it up in the Taj Mahal but Lola didn't want for anything.

'Please, Mirry.' Mal placed his hand on hers. 'I've not contributed at all and that's been very remiss of me. I want to do something.'

The earnestness in his gaze killed her objections. 'If you want to contribute then set up a bank account and start putting something away for her.'

Mal nodded. 'Yes. Good idea.' He reached across to his bedside table and grabbed his wallet, awkwardly retrieving a business card one-handed and passing it to her. 'And if she needs anything, or you need to get hold of me for any reason...'

Miranda nodded. 'Okay. Thanks. I will.'

When Miranda left a couple of minutes later the sense of relief was like a drug buzzing through her system.

She felt high.

Things *were* going to work out.

The feeling lasted until Friday night when the second whammy struck even more ferociously.

The divorce had come through that day and Patrick had taken them all out for an early dinner. Not even Helen's subdued mood throughout the meal could kill his elation. It was only natural that his mother-in-law would feel differently about the situation but after five years of living his life in limbo Patrick refused to let anything dampen his spirits.

He'd been in a holding pattern for so long he was looking forward to moving on.

As they were leaving the restaurant Lola, who was having a sleepover with Ruby, said, 'Are you coming back in the morning to pick me up, Mummy?'

'Nope,' Patrick announced. 'Your mummy is sleeping over too.'

Startled, Miranda glanced at him sharply. 'I am?'

He nodded. 'Sure you are.'

'But we don't have another bedroom, Daddy,' Ruby pointed out.

Patrick grinned at Ruby then grabbed Miranda, dipped her quickly and planted a quick, hard kiss on her mouth. 'She's sleeping in my bed,' he growled, before letting her go.

Miranda felt dizzy when he righted her and she wasn't entirely sure it had to do with the dip or the frank possession in his voice that was causing the earth to spin. They hadn't kissed in front of the girls before and Miranda checked on their reaction.

She needn't have worried.

Ruby and Lola were digging each other in the

ribs and giggling. Helen looked strangely resigned.

'Let's go,' Patrick said.

A couple of hours later the girls were asleep and Miranda and Patrick were watching a DVD in the lounge room. At least, Miranda was trying to. Patrick kept whispering all the outrageous things he was going to do to her when he got her to bed as he nuzzled her ear and his hand wandered up and down her thigh. Miranda, aware of Helen sitting at the table behind them at her sewing machine, was fending him off valiantly.

She felt sorry for Katie's mother, particularly today. How would she feel if Lola decided to cut her out of her life?

'Let's go to bed,' he murmured.

'It's only nine o'clock,' she whispered, shutting her eyes as his lips buzzed her jaw. If Helen hadn't been right there she'd have pushed him down on the lounge and had her way with him— hell, they wouldn't even be watching the damn movie. But she was and one of them had to be sensitive to their audience.

Patrick's fingers stroked up her leg. 'Move in with me,' he murmured.

Miranda slammed her hand down on his at it made for the inner seam of her jeans high on her thigh. She angled her neck to allow him better access as he dropped a kiss behind her ear. 'Patrick…' she sighed.

'You said, wait until after the divorce.' He raised his head and looked at her. 'I'm officially divorced.'

Miranda shook her head. 'How can I think straight when you play dirty?'

Patrick smiled against her neck. 'This isn't dirty,' he murmured, and tried to move his hand closer to the goalpost between her legs, but Miranda held it firmly in check.

'Patrick,' she said, her voice carrying a low warning as his teeth pressed against her skin and his whiskers scraped erotically along her collarbone. 'Maybe you need a cool drink?'

'No, I'm fine.'

Well *she* certainly needed one or she was going to pounce on him here and now, audience or not.

Miranda wiggled out of his clutches to a standing position. Her chest heaved in and out a little and he gave her a slow, lazy smile as he let his gaze drift all over her body.

She shook her head at him, smiling at his incorrigibility. 'I'll get us some,' she said, her voice warning him to behave.

She was halfway to the kitchen when the doorbell rang. Patrick frowned down at his watch. Helen looked up from the sewing machine.

'I'll go,' Miranda said, peeling off in the direction of the door, grateful for any time and space she could put between Patrick and her hormones before she got sucked back into the sexual force field that seemed to ooze from his every pore.

She opened the door, smiling as the memory of Patrick's lingering gaze titillated her way more than it should. A woman about her age stood at the door, the sensor light spilling down on a swathe of silky red hair burnishing the highlights into strands of golden thread. Miranda's smile died a quick death. She drew in a breath as the same feeling of foreboding she'd had while talking to Mal returned with vigour.

There was only one person this could be.

'Katie?' she said.

The woman frowned slightly but said, 'Yes,'

and then, 'I'm sorry. I know it's a little on the late side but I thought it would be best to come after I was sure Ruby would be down for the night.'

Miranda stood holding the screen door open, not taking any of it in, not moving. If she'd thought Mal's appearance had been a jolt, Katie's was like a lightning strike to her heart.

'Can I…can I come in?' she asked hesitantly. 'I'd like to talk to my mother…and Patrick.'

'Oh, yes, of course,' Miranda said, going into perfect hostess role even though the walls of her world were crashing down. She fell back and swept her hand in the direction of the lounge room. 'Through that way,' she said.

Miranda was right behind Katie when she entered the lounge room and was, as such, privy to Patrick and Helen's reactions. Helen burst into tears. Patrick's reaction was more measured. He ran a hand through his hair then shoved it on his hip as he stared at his wife.

Ex-wife.

Helen ran to her daughter and as Miranda made her way around the two of them, both women were crying and embracing. Patrick shifted his gaze to her and held out his arms. Miranda wanted nothing more than to walk into them, to feel their reassurance, but this, this…bomb blast was a game changer and she'd be stupid to think otherwise. So she avoided his embrace, dodged his gaze.

Patrick frowned at Miranda's evasion as Helen sobbed and hugged Katie. 'I can't believe you're here,' Helen blubbered. 'I thought this day would never come.'

'I'm so sorry, Mum,' Katie cried. 'I'm sorry I stayed away so long.'

Miranda turned to Patrick. 'I think I should go,' she said, gathering her hand bag off the lounge. She felt like an intruder in what should be a very private family reunion.

Patrick shook his head and grabbed her arm. 'No. You're staying. You belong here much more than she does.'

Miranda shivered at the steel in his voice that even reached the two sobbing women. 'Patrick!' Helen gasped.

'What? You can't be serious, Helen. Five years of desertion and you're just going to open your arms and forgive her for everything?'

'Of course not,' Helen said, dashing the tears

from her eyes. 'But if you don't mind, right this moment I'd like a little time to just be happy.'

'It's okay, Mum,' Katie said, swiping at her own tears. 'Patrick has every right to be furious. I owe him the biggest apology of all.'

Patrick could feel anger rising in him like a steaming kettle. She had *no freaking idea* how furious he was. 'No.' He snapped his back ramrod straight. 'You owe your daughter the biggest one of all.'

Katie teared up again. 'Yes,' she sniffled.

Patrick glared at her. She screwed up their lives and then just calmly waltzed back in after five years? 'What do you want, Katie?'

'Patrick…do we have to do this now?' Helen chided.

'Yes, Helen, we do. We really do. Katie's obviously shown up tonight for a reason.'

Miranda did not want to hear this. She tried to leave again but Patrick held fast to her arm.

'I've been trying to summon up the courage to come back for about six months now,' Katie said, her voice tremulous. 'I've been working on getting my head together for the last year or so. I took the divorce papers as a sign.'

Miranda blinked. What kind of sign? A re-alised-what-I'm-missing-out-on sign? A don't-really-want-it-to-be-over sign? Her heart beat so loudly Miranda was surprised no one else could hear it. She eased out of Patrick's grip and sank into the nearest chair because she wasn't sure how much longer her legs were going to support her.

Patrick snorted. 'The divorce papers weren't some open invitation to come back, Katie. They were closure. Our marriage is over.'

'I'm not talking about a sign for us, for our rela-tionship. I'm talking about Ruby. About building a relationship with her. About being her mother.'

Patrick felt the steam burn and boil as his blood pressure hit the roof. 'Oh, so you want to be her *mother* now, do you?'

Katie took a step back as his anger blasted over her with the full force of a roadside bomb. 'I don't expect it to happen overnight…but, yes, I want to start reconnecting with her…'

For the first time in his life Patrick understood what people said when they talked about seeing red. It blurred his vision and he blinked hard to shift it. A cold mist descended over him, freezing out any ounce of compassion.

'Over. My. Dead. Body.'

'Patrick,' Helen said reproachfully, as more tears squeezed out of Katie's eyes.

'I'm happy to go slowly, to do it on your terms,' Katie said quietly. 'For you to set the agenda.'

He shook his head. 'No.'

Katie clutched her mother's arm hard and swallowed.

'Okay, maybe we all need a little time to adjust. I'll go—for now. But I want to talk again when you've calmed down, work out a way forward.'

Patrick couldn't believe what he was hearing. She turned up after five years, he didn't know the first thing about who she was now or even if she was capable of looking after a five-year-old, and she just expected him to hand over to her the most precious thing in the world to him?

'You can talk to my lawyer.'

Helen whimpered as tears sprang to her eyes again and Katie patted her hand. 'You need to know that I'm not going anywhere, Patrick. I made some mistakes that I can't take back but I *am* her mother and I'm here to make up for lost time, to be a permanent part of her life, so you're going to have to deal with me.'

Patrick shook his head at her audacity. She was going to throw her rights in his face? 'Get out,' he said.

Miranda shivered at the menace in his tone. She'd only ever known Patrick to be laid back. This Patrick was deadly serious.

'Where are you staying, darling?' Helen asked.

'I've checked into a caravan park with some cabins for a few days,' Katie said. 'Do you want to come back with me?'

Helen hugged her daughter hard. 'Of course.' She looked at Patrick. 'Is that okay?'

Patrick wanted to break things. Since when had Helen needed to ask his permission for anything? 'You're not my indentured servant, Helen,' he snapped. 'You can do whatever you want.'

Helen ignored the tone and tugged on her daughter's arm. 'Come with me while I throw some things into a bag.'

Silence reigned, thick and heavy, as Miranda watched Patrick prowl around the lounge room for the five minutes it took for Helen and Katie to leave the house. The door shut after them and he collapsed back into the lounge chair, raking his hands through his hair. He looked like he'd been punched when he finally turned his troubled autumn gaze her way.

'Un-freaking-believable,' he said.

Miranda wanted to go to him, to fold him in her arms and tell him it was all going to be okay, but she wasn't sure it would be. Not for her and him anyway, and she could already feel herself pulling back, curling in on herself emotionally, like she had as a child every time her father had walked out the door again.

'It was always on the cards that she'd come back someday,' Miranda said gently.

Her quiet truth drained Patrick of his anger in an instant. Yes, he'd known it too. But today, of all days? Talk about raining on his parade! He sat forward in his chair, leaning his elbows on his knees. 'It doesn't mean she can waltz in and start demanding things,' he said wearily.

Miranda nodded. 'If it's any consolation, I don't think she wants to do that.'

Patrick looked at her. 'It sounds like you're on her side.'

Miranda felt a shiver down her spine as he

evoked echoes from her childhood. Already there was talk of sides. Which side would Lola chose? 'She's Ruby's mother, Patrick.'

'Who walked out on her when she was *six weeks old?*' he fumed.

Miranda nodded. 'I know. I know. But if she really wants to come back in and can prove she's willing and able...' Even the thought broke Miranda's heart. 'I don't think it would be wise to deny her that.'

Patrick didn't want to hear reason. Not tonight. Tonight he wanted to be angry. 'So you're allowed to deny Mal contact with Lola but I'm not allowed to do the same with Katie?'

'It's not the same situation and you know it,' Miranda said, reaching for calmness that she did not feel. 'You were married to Katie. She grew Ruby inside her and she gave birth to her, and even though she left she would have formed a bond with Ruby in those months.'

Part of Miranda felt for Katie even if she didn't understand her. How had she coped without seeing her daughter for all those years?

'Also not forgetting you have an ongoing existing close relationship with Katie's mother, as does Ruby with her grandmother. I had none of that with Mal. He was nothing more than a… sperm donor. Katie was your wife and Ruby's mother, no matter how briefly, and that's a huge difference.'

And it didn't bode well for her.

'And if Mal had insisted, I wouldn't have denied him, and I really don't think you can deny Katie or Ruby a chance at a relationship, Patrick. Not without it backfiring on you badly. And, as a mother, I would be disappointed in you if you did.'

Miranda stood then because although she believed every word she'd just said, that working out an arrangement with Katie was the right thing to do, it didn't mean it was easy to say.

'I'm going,' she said.

She needed to step back and give Patrick and Katie time to sort out what came next. And if she stayed tonight she wasn't sure if she'd be strong enough to walk away.

Patrick stood too. 'No, don't… Please stay.' If there was ever a night he needed to be with the woman he loved, to ground himself, to reassure himself, it was tonight. 'I need you.'

Miranda squeezed back the tears that pricked like poison darts at her eyes. He reached for her again and she sidestepped him, pulling back emotionally as well as physically.

'I can't,' she said, looking at him, silently begging him to see that walking away was hard for her as well. 'I need to think. So do you.'

Patrick raked a hand through his hair. 'Nothing has to change, Miranda. Not if we don't let it.'

She gave him a sad smile. He was too smart not to know that *everything* had changed. 'Sometimes we don't get a choice,' she murmured.

And she walked away on wobbly legs.

CHAPTER ELEVEN

PATRICK LOOKED AS if he hadn't slept a wink when Miranda dropped round the next morning to pick Lola up. Which made two of them. So this time when he held his arms out to her she didn't resist, allowing herself to sink into them, to hold him one more time.

He felt solid and smelled like coffee and chocolate Cocoa Pops and she didn't want to let him go, but she was thankful for the umpteenth time she hadn't allowed herself to fall in love with him. To have let herself go there. Last night would have utterly destroyed her had she been in love with him. There was only a certain number of times a girl could be knocked down before she never got up again.

'Still pissed off?' she asked him with a slight smile as she pulled away.

He gave a grudging smile of his own. 'Yep.'

Miranda watched as he poured her a coffee and

when she took it from him she was careful they didn't come into contact. They took the drinks out to the back deck and she was conscious of him behind her all the way.

'So,' she said as she sat at the table, waving to Lola as the girls played in the sandpit, 'did you come to any conclusions last night? Got a plan?'

Patrick shrugged. His eyes felt gritty and just thinking about the situation was enough to give him a headache. 'I need to talk to my lawyer on Monday, first.'

An itch worked up Miranda's spine and she was torn between what she wanted to say and what was the right thing to say. She didn't want to be the one to tell him what to do with his ex-wife. To be the nagger like her mother had been with her father about his wife—she didn't want that relationship with him.

But she didn't want him to stuff things up either. For himself or for Ruby.

'Do you think threatening her with legal action is the best foot to put forward in the first instance? Do you really want to alienate her from the get-go? Alienate Helen?'

'I'm not talking about legal action. I just want to know my rights. Her rights. It's just…advice.'

They watched the girls playing for a while, drinking their coffee in silence. Patrick glanced at Miranda surreptitiously. She'd always held herself back a bit and he understood why, but still he'd known that, underneath it all, her feelings for him ran deep and true.

But overnight she seemed to have withdrawn even more.

'I meant what I said last night,' he murmured.

Miranda's fingers tightened around her coffee mug. She took a second to gather herself before she looked at him and played dumb. 'What did you say?'

'Nothing has to change with us. I still love you. I still want you and Lola to move in. I still want us to be a family.'

Miranda felt his words ping against her heart, each one a tiny little bullet drawing blood.

'Patrick…' She shook her head and battled the tears she'd refused to let fall all night and which she'd be damned if she'd let fall now. Someone had to be the voice of reason here and it looked like it was going to be her.

'I'm not getting into something with the two of us when all this other…*stuff,* this really big, really important stuff, is going on around the edges. It would be too…fraught.'

Patrick reached for her hand. 'It doesn't have to be.'

Miranda pulled her hand away with a supreme effort. 'It's going to be nigh on impossible to so-lidify our relationship as a couple when you're trying to establish a relationship—'

Patrick slammed down his coffee cup. 'I am not interested in a relationship with Katie,' he snapped.

'Oh, don't be naïve,' Miranda hissed. 'You're going to have one whether you like it or not. For crying out loud, you *already* have one. This isn't about what you and I want any more. You have to make this as easy for Ruby as possible.'

Patrick put his elbows on the table and ruffled his hair. He knew she was right but, for cry-ing out loud, when would he get a chance to be happy? 'And when do we get our turn?'

His eyes were bleak as he asked the question and they twisted through Miranda's gut. 'We're parents. We put our kids' needs first. That's what we do. You and I have spent five years making Ruby and Lola our priorities and you can't duck out of it now. *Especially* now. Ruby's world's going to change, she's going to suddenly have a *mother* again, and she's going to be looking at you for her cues, for reassurance.'

'And you don't think you could help ease that transition too?'

Of course she could, but the real question was whether she could bear to live through Ruby's inevitable anxiety. Because there would be anxiety—that was just Ruby's personality. And it would strike just a little too close to home for her.

'I think it's going to be confusing enough without having two *mothers* around.'

Patrick could feel himself getting more and more desperate. He needed Miranda now more than ever. 'We'd have had to deal with it if this had happened two years down the track.'

'Yes. But it's not two years down the track, is it? So we have a choice now. One that we can make carefully with wisdom and by putting *Ruby* first. And being thankful that it happened now, before we got in too deep.'

Thankful? Patrick saw red again.

Maybe at some stage in the future, if everything ran smoothly, he'd be thankful that Ruby knew her mother, but he would *never* be happy about the torpedo that had blasted their relationship apart.

And he didn't believe for a moment that Miranda did either. She may not have ever told him she loved him, but he didn't doubt for a minute that she did. He understood that her past had made her wary but he was sick of her hiding behind it.

'Before we got in too deep?' He stood, his pulse roaring in his ears, his chair scraping on the wooden deck and then toppling backwards with the force. 'That's what this is about, isn't it? Not about Ruby and her needs but about you and protecting yourself before you get in too deep!'

Miranda shot a quick glance at the girls, who had looked up when the chair had banged and were both looking at them curiously.

'It's like you had this perfect fairy-tale in your head of how family life should be. But no family is perfect, Miranda. They all go through their ups and downs. You want what doesn't exist.'

Miranda's temper flared at his accusation and

she forgot the girls were there. She didn't want perfection but she wanted as close as she could get to it. For her but especially for Lola. She wanted Lola to have what she hadn't had growing up—not more of the same.

'You're wrong,' she snarled. 'It's out there and I'm prepared to wait for it!'

Patrick could feel it all slipping away and he wanted to reach across the table and shake her. Instead, he slammed his fist down with a thunk. The coffee cup rattled and tipped on its side with a harsh clatter.

'It's not!' he yelled. 'Face it, nothing will ever live up to your expectations.'

Miranda opened her mouth to tell him to go to hell but a plaintive little voice broke into their argument.

'Daddy?'

They both turned, facing their audience. The girls had moved closer. Ruby was nibbling on her lip and twisting her fingers in her T-shirt. Lola had her arms around Ruby's neck, a frown marring her forehead.

'Stop yelling at my mummy,' Lola ordered in

her little sergeant-major voice as she glared at Patrick.

A wave of nausea accompanied the sense of déjà vu that slammed into Miranda and she was pleased she was sitting. The tension was starting already. The choosing of sides. Patrick seemed to be temporarily speechless and she forced herself to her feet and plastered a smile on her face.

'It's fine, Lols,' she said, nodding reassuringly at her daughter and forcing herself to extend the smile to Patrick for the girls' sake. 'We're just having a bit of a disagreement but we're fine, aren't we, Patrick?'

Patrick followed Miranda's cue, although he was still poleaxed by the situation. Ruby looked more worried than he'd seen her in a long time. Her anxiety had settled dramatically over the last six months. And fiery little Lola, sweeping in to defend her mother and comfort Ruby, was a sight to behold.

'Of course,' he assured her, also smiling but going one further, joining Miranda round the other side of the table, putting his arm around her shoulder and pulling her into his side. 'We're fine.'

The smile hurt Miranda's face but she kept it up as she spoke to the girls. Even with everything all wrong, just being close to him somehow seemed right and it was an effort to keep her head held high instead of burying it in his shoulder, like she wanted to. 'Okey-dokey, Lols, time to go. Grab your stuff.'

'Oh, but, Mum—' Lola started to protest.

'No buts,' Miranda interrupted, probably a little more sharply than she should have if Lola's puzzled expression was anything to go by. 'We're busy, busy today so hop to it! Make sure you brush the sand off your feet before you go in the house.'

For a moment Lola looked like she was going to protest some more but she thought better of it and the girls headed inside. As soon as they'd skipped by, Miranda stepped out of the circle of Patrick's arms.

She looked up into his face and waited until his gaze was locked with hers before she said a word. 'This is what I don't want,' she said. 'I don't want to live with tension and friction and I don't want Lola to be dragged into it either. That's how I grew up and I *do not* want it for my life now or the life of my daughter.'

Patrick shook his head. 'So let's make a promise to not do it that way.'

Miranda shut out the reasoned note in his voice. He didn't know how hard it was to blend families. She did. 'Easier said than done.'

Patrick dug his fingers into his waist as the urge to shake her grew. 'Let's just give it a try,' he pleaded.

Miranda picked up her mug. 'It's not a risk I'm prepared to take with my kid. And you shouldn't be prepared to either.'

He snorted. 'Isn't loving someone worth the risk? Isn't it better to have loved and lost?'

Miranda shook her head as she looked into the cold leftovers of her coffee. Her mother would say yes but as a casualty of her love Miranda begged to differ. She glanced at him. 'Not when there's children involved.'

And then she pulled away, walked into the house and called for Lola, and when she drove away five minutes later she felt awful but Lola's smile in the rear-view mirror warmed her heart.

* * *

The next weeks were difficult. Miranda and Patrick saw each other at work constantly and worked side by side often. Adjusting to their new status in such an enclosed environment wasn't easy. They'd just got used to all the gossip and speculation about them and now they were back to denying their relationship again.

Still, one well-timed conversation with Lilly ensured that the entire theatre staff were up to speed, which helped to ease the transition.

Other than enquiring each day how things were going 'at home' and Patrick replying with a terse 'Fine', they kept their conversations strictly about work. About what size ETT he wanted or which fluid to hang or which drug to draw up. About allergies and difficult airways and hard-to-place IVs.

Trying to carry on as normal in front of the girls was the most difficult. Luckily Miranda had insisted that they not be openly affectionate or demonstrative over the previous months so they were able to carry on as they always had with each other without the girls figuring something was up. They just did fewer things together as a foursome.

She often still picked Ruby up from school for Patrick and the girls still had play dates but the focus was on Ruby and Lola getting together, not all of them getting together as a unit. Miranda and Patrick dropped and picked up but never stayed or lingered.

And Miranda was pretty sure they hadn't noticed. Certainly not Lola anyway, who was as oblivious as usual to anything outside her own existence.

A month after their separation Miranda was allocated to Patrick's morning theatre list and the butterflies she always felt when she had to work with him and pretend that he wasn't the best lover she'd ever known turned to pterodactyls clawing at the inside of her stomach as Patrick's thunderous mood grabbed hold and shook everyone who came close. Even his famous ease with the patients was a little worn around the edges.

He looked like he hadn't slept all night and not even his sexy pink scrubs were endearing him to anyone.

'Okay, Patrick,' she said as she stormed into

the anaesthetic room between patients. 'What the hell is wrong with you?'

Patrick turned as her anger practically reached out and yanked him round. It was on the tip of his tongue to tell her to stay out of his business but her big green eyes stroked something inside him and what he really wanted to do was to grab hold of her and never let her go.

But she'd made it clear that wasn't an option.

He sagged against the bench, the fight draining out of him. 'Nothing,' he sighed, lifting his hand to his forehead and massaging his temples briefly. 'Katie is coming for tea tonight... Ruby's going to be meeting her for the first time and I feel so sick about it I'm taking it out on everyone else.'

Miranda nodded. Lola had casually announced last night that Ruby's real mummy was coming to tea. She'd tried to gently probe Lola for more information but Lola was her usual egocentric self and it just felt wrong to dig.

'This is a big first step,' she said. 'It's a taken a while to get there.'

Patrick nodded. 'I told Katie she had to be settled here first, get a job, prove to me that she was going to stick around and then we'd talk about her being involved with Ruby.' He grimaced. 'She had a market stall gig and Helen helped her rent a small flat four suburbs away within three weeks.'

'Ah.' Miranda understood. 'You thought you'd have longer.'

'Yep.'

'Well…that's good, right?' she enquired gently. 'She's trying to prove to you that she's serious.'

'Yep.'

'Have you guys come up with some kind of plan?'

Patrick shifted against the bench behind him. 'Weekly visits for a while, tea at my place, until Ruby gets to know Katie better. Then a Saturday outing together, Katie and Ruby and Helen.'

'Oh, it's good that Helen will be there.'

'Yes. I feel better about that. And then…' he shrugged '…we'll see. Katie's being very amenable.'

Miranda heard the grudging respect and tried not to read any more into it. 'Has she…has Katie talked about what happened? Why she took off?' Miranda asked.

She knew she didn't have any right to ask and

he had every right to tell her to mind her own business, but she couldn't contain her curiosity.

'She said she had a bit of breakdown. Post-natal depression. That when she walked out that day she was in a total fugue state. She doesn't even remember that she rang one of her old party friends who picked her up and they camped out on a beach near Byron Bay for two weeks. When she discovered that people thought she was missing, possibly murdered, she made that phone call.'

Miranda blinked. It was a hard situation to comprehend. Katie had obviously needed medical help. 'And then what?'

'She reckons she went into a state of denial, convinced herself that because she didn't have any feelings for her baby that Ruby was better off without her.'

'So she just…dropped out?'

'Pretty much. She reverted to her maiden name, blocked me, our marriage and Ruby out, and she and a few other hippy types just travelled around, getting jobs where they could. Fruit picking. Busking. Living hand to mouth. It's where she rediscovered her artistic side and got into portrait sketching.'

'So…did she have some kind of epiphany recently?'

Patrick folded his arms and crossed one ankle over the other. 'One of her friends got pregnant and she started having flashbacks. They were in Darwin and she started seeing a shrink and had therapy for almost a year. She's on medication now and has already hooked up with a local psychologist the Darwin guy recommended.'

Miranda felt strangely teary. She was happy that Katie seemed to have got her life together. Happy for her and for Ruby. 'Well, I'm sure tonight's going to go okay. Katie's obviously keen to make a good impression.'

Patrick knew that but he knew after tonight things would never be the same and frankly it scared him senseless. For so long he'd only known one way to parent and now he had to embrace another. 'I'm sure it will,' he murmured, as much for his own benefit as hers.

And then the phone rang to let Miranda know the next patient was at the entrance and they both went back to their corners.

* * *

A month later Miranda knocked on Patrick's door one Friday afternoon to drop Lola off for a sleepover. She was expecting Helen so it was a shock when Katie answered the door.

'Oh…hi,' Miranda said as Lola gave her a quick hug around her waist then raced inside with Ruby.

Miranda was struck by how much Ruby looked like her mother. It was uncanny.

'Hi.' Katie smiled. 'I'm sorry, we haven't met officially yet.' She held out her hand. 'It's nice to meet you, Miranda. Mum's told me a lot about you.'

Miranda's heart raced, not entirely sure that was good news. She and Helen had always got along but she'd known Helen had found Patrick's burgeoning relationship with her difficult.

'I'm just here for tea,' Katie said hastily. 'Why don't you come in? Patrick should be home soon. Actually, why don't you stay for tea?'

Miranda shook her head, knowing that it would be too difficult to watch the Patrick and Katie show. 'Oh, no, I don't want to…intrude. I'll be back in the morning to pick up Lola.'

'No, wait, please,' Katie said, putting her hand

on Miranda's arm. 'Stay. You should stay.' Katie hesitated for a moment. 'It was never my intention to create trouble for you and Patrick. Blind Freddy can see that he loves you. And he deserves to be happy. I'm sure we could sit down and work it all out if we really tried.'

Miranda believed her. But this wasn't what she wanted. She didn't want to be in a relationship that was complicated and messy and weighed down by baggage. She'd escaped that and she wasn't going back again.

She pulled away. 'No…I'm sorry…I'm very happy for you…and for Ruby but…'

Katie gave her a gentle smile. 'You love him too. I can see it in your eyes.'

'No.' She shook her head. 'No.' She didn't. She hadn't let herself go there. 'I…have to go… Tell Lola I'll pick her up at ten.'

She didn't wait for a reply. She just turned away and headed for the car and home, far away from Katie's ridiculous notion.

By the time Monday came around Miranda felt like she was holding back a tidal wave inside her. Her head pounded, her stomach was screwed in a knot so tight she doubted even the most experienced sailor would be able to undo it, and her heart felt like a boulder in her chest.

Katie's words had reverberated round and round her head all weekend. *You love him too.*

No.

No, no, no.

She couldn't love him. She just wouldn't allow it.

She was grateful Patrick had a day off today because running into him would have been too, too much. He'd been in her head solidly for the last forty-eight hours and she'd had enough.

She refused to think about him any more.

She refused to love him.

And she refused to cry about it.

She was going to spend eight blissful hours absorbed with important things like life and death. Things she had control over. Things she could do something about.

And Patrick Costello be damned.

That worked really well until the last case, an emergency Caesarean section.

Miranda loved these cases best. There was a hum of expectation in the air that infected everyone. Even more so if the mother was having an epidural and had her partner in tow.

There was nothing better than that moment when the baby first cried and everyone in the operating theatre who'd been holding their breaths finally smiled. You couldn't see them beneath the masks, but they were the types of smiles that went all the way to the eyes.

Witnessing a new life coming into the world was always magical.

It was true goose-bump material.

Miranda sat at the head of the operating table with the couple as the surgeons draped and prepped. In this situation it was her job to talk the couple through each stage of the operation, keep them calm and focussed while the anaesthetist managed the epidural.

'Girl or boy, do you know?' Miranda asked.

'Little girl,' Diane, the mother, confirmed, adjusting her nasal prongs.

'Little Faith,' Darryl, the father, confirmed. He was dressed in scrubs and a mask and cap like everyone else and holding his wife's hand tightly. 'She may have her problems but she's our little blessing in disguise and we love her.'

He kissed Diane gently on the forehead as Miranda surreptitiously checked the chart. The baby had been diagnosed on amniocentesis as having Down's syndrome.

Diane smiled at her husband as the surgeon announced he was making the first incision. 'We're so lucky,' she said. 'We gave up on life for a while there with Darryl's cancer coming back so soon after his remission, but then we thought, screw it, love's a gift, right?'

Miranda watched with a lump in her throat as Darryl stroked Diane's face and she beamed at him. She felt a huge crack in the boulder in her chest.

'So we got married and we got pregnant and we'll just take every day as it comes. Things aren't perfect but there aren't any guarantees in life, are there, so why not be happy while you can?'

Miranda blinked back threatening tears. She could hear the sucker in the background suctioning away the amniotic fluid but it felt as if it was sucking out the knot in her stomach, splitting her belly wide open.

Before her were two people who had been

through the mill. Darryl had cancer with what sounded like a poor prognosis and they were about to welcome a new baby who had Down's syndrome.

Their lives were hard and imperfect and messy and complicated. But they could still love.

And five minutes later, when little Faith's lusty first cry sliced through the expectant hush, Miranda finally let go of what she'd been holding back for so long.

She loved Patrick.

She loved him.

And it wasn't like the impetuousness she'd experienced with Mal. Or the desperate, girlish desire to play house with Neil. It was just there, sure and steady and real. Like her breath. Like her heartbeat.

And it was hard and imperfect and messy and complicated, and she suddenly didn't care.

Diane was crying, Darryl was crying and she joined them.

An hour later she'd texted Patrick to tell him she'd pick Ruby up from school. And half an hour after that she was on his doorstep, the girls tear-ing inside and heading straight for the kitchen and the smell of baking biscuits that had wafted out to greet them.

'Do you want to come in?' Helen asked as Miranda hovered on the doorstep.

'Is Patrick here?'

'He's out in the back yard, doing some mulching.' She smiled. 'Why don't you go on through?'

Miranda nodded, suddenly nervous. It was great to see Helen so happy and relaxed now but it just seemed to amplify her own nerves. She entered the house and slowly made her way through to the back. She'd been so busy with the logistics of getting to his place as fast as possible that she hadn't given a lot of thought to what she was going to say.

What if she'd blown it with him?

She followed the path that led to the sandpit and there he was, shovelling mulch from a wheelbarrow onto a garden bed. It was a warm day and the sun glistened on beads of sweat on his neck, forehead and forearms, his shirt stuck to the small of his back.

It wasn't pink scrubs but it was sexy and earthy and her heart broke open even more.

She didn't say anything for a moment. Just watched him, drank in the sight of him. The firm muscles in his arms not contained by his T-shirt bunched with each movement, as did the thick slabs of his quadriceps.

'Hello, Patrick,' she called.

Patrick turned to find Miranda in loose yoga-style pants and a T-shirt standing in his yard. For a moment he thought he was hallucinating. That she was a mirage shimmering in the sun conjured up by his overactive imagination because, God knew, he'd thought of her almost constantly these last couple of months.

But then she smiled at him and he knew she was real. 'Miranda?'

Miranda panicked. What could she say to make up for abandoning him when things had got tough? For chickening out when he'd needed her? 'I've been an idiot,' she said.

Patrick held his ground. 'Yes.'

Miranda gave a half-laugh. 'You're hell on a girl's ego.'

Patrick wasn't sure what she was doing there, looking at him with eyes that seemed to say things that she'd been denying for months. But whatever it was, she should just cut to the chase. 'What do you want, Miranda?'

Miranda's smile died as his voice left her in no doubt this was not the time for jokes. 'You.'

Her voice wobbled and she cleared her throat. 'I've been trying to deny how I've felt about you for months and months and months because I was too scared to take a risk on anything that wasn't perfect. I'm sorry. I know my childhood kind of messed me up but, God, Patrick…it really was hell and I didn't want that for Lola, and I guess that affected me more than I ever really knew, and you and our relationship were a casualty of that. Another casualty.'

He was just standing there looking at her and she wished he'd say something.

'I knew that you loved me but I couldn't let myself feel that for you. I couldn't risk it because ever since I was little I wanted to have a man sweep me away and live in his castle with him happily ever after, and the version you were offering, our version of that, was not romantic or perfect and I was determined to reject it.'

Silence. He was just watching her.

'But today…today my heart cracked open like

a big fault line and the love I've been hiding from came gushing out. And I can't stop it, it just keeps filling me and filling me and filling me.'

Still he said nothing.

'Patrick,' she begged. 'Please say something.'

Patrick didn't want to say a word. He wanted to sweep her up into his arms and kiss her until they were both breathless, but he had the feeling she had more on her mind. 'What happened to change your mind today?'

'A patient,' she said. 'A couple in for a Caesarean who have this messy, complicated life but who chose love anyway. And when that little baby girl cried it was like she unlocked everything I'd been hoarding away because I was too frightened to try.'

He didn't say anything to that but that was okay because Miranda wasn't finished. 'I know my mother botched it up. So did my father. But *we* don't have to, right? We can make it work. With us and the girls and Katie and Helen and Nan. I know it won't be easy but if we all work together we can blend this family and do it well, right?'

Still nothing and finally his impassiveness was

getting on her last nerve because she was really starting to think she had blown it.

'God, please tell me I'm right, Patrick,' she begged, her voice husky and cracking right at the end as a tear slipped from her eye.

For a moment he didn't say or do anything and then he smiled at her and then he was striding towards her and pulling her into his arms and wrapping them around her.

'Of course you're right,' he said, his lips brushing her hair. 'It won't be perfect, but we'll make it work because we love each other and we're committed to making it work.'

Miranda swallowed hard against the massive swelling in her throat as more tears threatened. 'Oh, God, Patrick, you had me so worried.' She pulled back slightly. 'I'm so sorry I've been such an idiot. I thought for an awful moment you were going to tell me you didn't love me any more.'

Patrick smiled down at Miranda, his heart so big in his chest he thought it might just burst through his ribcage. 'From the day you dropped Pinky in the lift until right now I have loved you.' He dropped a light kiss on the corner of her mouth. 'Even if you are an idiot.'

And then he grinned and kissed her again. And again and again. And it wasn't until they heard two little giggles that they broke apart. 'Are you going to marry my mummy?' Lola asked.

Patrick nodded. 'Yes, I am.'

The girls clapped and cheered, jumping up and down like they had springs on their feet. Ruby turned to look at Lola. '*Now* can we be flower-girlth?' she asked.

'Can we, Mummy?' Lola asked, shifting from foot to foot.

'Yes,' Miranda said. 'That would be perfect.'

And she smiled at Patrick as the girls ran to them and she embraced her different kind of perfect.

EPILOGUE

Five years later...

PATRICK LOOKED AT his very pregnant wife as the expected knock came at the expected time. Three-year-old Harrison who was drifting off to sleep on Patrick's shoulder raised his sleepy head and said, 'Door.'

Patrick kissed his son's forehead. 'Yes, someone's at the door,' he said absently as he watched Miranda nervously twisting her rings around and around her finger.

'I'll get it,' Katie called from the lounge room.

Patrick ignored it. 'You okay?' he asked.

Miranda nodded. 'Of course. I'm just nervous for Lola.'

Her gaze fell on the framed picture sitting on their bedside table of Lola and Ruby both resplendent in frothy pink dresses, wreaths of flowers in their hair, grinning at the camera almost five years ago. They'd all come a long way in that time but their girls were still inseparable.

'He's here,' Katie said arriving in the bedroom doorway. 'I took him through to the lounge. The table is set and I can serve up lunch whenever you're ready.'

'Where's Lola?' Patrick asked.

'She and Ruby are still deciding what she should wear. I'll hurry them along.'

Miranda smiled gratefully at Katie. 'Thanks.' If someone had told her five years ago that they'd all be living together—including Nan—in one big old house she'd have laughed. It felt a lot like she'd been plonked into the set of the Brady Bunch but somehow it just worked and Miranda wouldn't have it any other way.

Patrick wandered over to Miranda and pulled her in close to his body with his spare arm. He dropped a kiss on her neck, his chest filling with love, his hand running over the round contours of her belly.

'Mummy,' Harrison murmured, reaching out a hand to touch her too.

Miranda smiled and kissed his little hand as

Lola and Ruby appeared in the doorway then joined them for a hug.

'Are we all ready?' Patrick asked after a minute and was greeted with a murmur of affirmation.

Miranda squeezed Lola's hand and smiled at her. 'Let's go meet your dad.'

And they headed out of the room to meet their next challenge, as a family.

* * * * *

Mills & Boon® *Large Print*
Medical

January

DR DARK AND FAR-TOO DELICIOUS	Carol Marinelli
SECRETS OF A CAREER GIRL	Carol Marinelli
THE GIFT OF A CHILD	Sue MacKay
HOW TO RESIST A HEARTBREAKER	Louisa George
A DATE WITH THE ICE PRINCESS	Kate Hardy
THE REBEL WHO LOVED HER	Jennifer Taylor

February

MIRACLE ON KAIMOTU ISLAND	Marion Lennox
ALWAYS THE HERO	Alison Roberts
THE MAVERICK DOCTOR AND MISS PRIM	Scarlet Wilson
ABOUT THAT NIGHT...	Scarlet Wilson
DARING TO DATE DR CELEBRITY	Emily Forbes
RESISTING THE NEW DOC IN TOWN	Lucy Clark

March

THE WIFE HE NEVER FORGOT	Anne Fraser
THE LONE WOLF'S CRAVING	Tina Beckett
SHELTERED BY HER TOP-NOTCH BOSS	Joanna Neil
RE-AWAKENING HIS SHY NURSE	Annie Claydon
A CHILD TO HEAL THEIR HEARTS	Dianne Drake
SAFE IN HIS HANDS	Amy Ruttan

Mills & Boon® Large Print
Medical

April

GOLD COAST ANGELS: A DOCTOR'S REDEMPTION	Marion Lennox
GOLD COAST ANGELS: TWO TINY HEARTBEATS	Fiona McArthur
CHRISTMAS MAGIC IN HEATHERDALE	Abigail Gordon
THE MOTHERHOOD MIX-UP	Jennifer Taylor
THE SECRET BETWEEN THEM	Lucy Clark
CRAVING HER ROUGH DIAMOND DOC	Amalie Berlin

May

GOLD COAST ANGELS: BUNDLE OF TROUBLE	Fiona Lowe
GOLD COAST ANGELS: HOW TO RESIST TEMPTATION	Amy Andrews
HER FIREFIGHTER UNDER THE MISTLETOE	Scarlet Wilson
SNOWBOUND WITH DR DELECTABLE	Susan Carlisle
HER REAL FAMILY CHRISTMAS	Kate Hardy
CHRISTMAS EVE DELIVERY	Connie Cox

June

FROM VENICE WITH LOVE	Alison Roberts
CHRISTMAS WITH HER EX	Fiona McArthur
AFTER THE CHRISTMAS PARTY...	Janice Lynn
HER MISTLETOE WISH	Lucy Clark
DATE WITH A SURGEON PRINCE	Meredith Webber
ONCE UPON A CHRISTMAS NIGHT...	Annie Claydon